MISSION 7

COUNTDOWN

mars
DIARIES

MISSION 7

COUNTDOWN

SIGMUND BROUWER

TYNDALE HOUSE PUBLISHERS, INC.
WHEATON, ILLINOIS

Visit Tyndale's exciting Web site for kids at www.marsdiaries.com

Helicopter image rendered by Ron Kaufmann.

Designed by Justin Ahrens and Ron Kaufmann

Edited by Ramona Cramer Tucker

ISBN 0-8423-4310-5

Printed in the United States of America

07 06 05 04 03 02 01
7   6   5   4   3   2   1

CHAPTER 1

Neuron rifles.

Twenty soldiers—in full protective gear, including black uniforms, black helmets, dark mirrored visors—each held a rifle, aimed directly at my head. The voltage of just one neuron rifle would cripple me with the pain of an electrical jolt through the nerve pathways of my body.

But 20 neuron rifles fired at me all at once? With the nerve pathways too scrambled to give instructions to my muscles, I wouldn't even be able to scream as I died.

Each of those soldiers followed my slow progress by keeping me in the sights of their weapons. I had nowhere to run. Nowhere to hide.

Only moments earlier, the robot that carried me in its arms had arrived to take me out of my prison cell. I'd grabbed my comp-board—my fold-up laptop computer—in the few seconds I had to gather my belongings. I had left behind my wheelchair from Mars, since it was useless. The prison officials had removed its wheels on the remote chance I'd find a way to escape. Now as the robot wheeled down the wide white corridor of this military prison, the soldiers flanked me, front and back.

Carried as I was by the robot, I felt like a baby. Worse, if the robot set me down, the best I'd be able to do was crawl by using my arms to pull me forward. I was without my wheelchair, and after a lifetime on Mars, I struggled with the extra gravity on Earth.

The squeak of the robot's wheels provided a steady backdrop to the soft thumping of the soldiers' footsteps in the quiet of the corridor. None of the soldiers spoke. I wondered if they would fire without warning. I wondered how long they would let the robot continue to take me away from my prison cell. I wondered why they had let me go this far.

I wondered where I was going. And why.

All I knew was that the robot had appeared as my prison cell door opened, and that from the speakers of the robot, a familiar but mechanical-sounding voice had instructed me to sit up from my bunk so that the robot's arms could lift me. I had trusted that voice.

And now I was here.

With all those neuron rifles ready and able to kill me in the worst way possible.

I didn't know why I'd been put in this prison. Two days ago Chase Sanders, my dad and the pilot of the *Moon Racer* spaceship, my friend Ashley, and I had arrived from Mars—where I had been born over 14 Earth years ago. To our shock World United Federation soldiers had boarded our ship and arrested us. And I hadn't talked to Ashley or my dad since.

In my solitude, I kept wondering if it had anything to do with the robots.

For about as long as I could remember, I had been trained in a virtual-reality program. Like the ones on Earth where you put on a surround-sight helmet that gives you a three-dimensional view of a scene on a computer program. The helmet is wired so that when you turn your head, it directs the computer program to shift the scene as if you were there in real life. Sounds come in like real sounds. Because you're wearing a wired jacket and gloves, the arms and hands you see in your surround-sight picture move wherever you move your own arms and hands.

With me, the only difference is that the wiring reaches my brain directly through my spine. And I can control a real robot, not one in virtual reality. You see, part of the long-term Mars Project that my mom, dad, and I were a part of was to use robots—which don't need oxygen, water, or heat—to explore Mars. However, the problem was that robots couldn't think like humans.

And that's where I came in. When I was a baby, I had an experimental operation to insert a special rod with thousands of tiny, biological implant fibers into my spine. Each of the fibers has a core that transmits tiny impulses of electricity, allowing my brain to control a robot's computer. From all my years of training in a computer simulation program, my mind knows all the muscle moves it takes to handle the virtual-reality controls. Handling the robot is no different, except instead of actually moving my muscles, I imagine I'm moving the muscles. My brain sends the proper nerve impulses to the robot, and it moves the way I made the robot move in the virtual-reality computer program.

I admit, it's cool. Almost worth being in a wheelchair.

Ashley was wired in the same way—with one difference. Because she'd had the operation on Earth, with better medical facilities, her spine hadn't been damaged. She had the best of both worlds.

Now she was controlling the robot that was carrying me.

Only I had no idea how she'd gotten control of it.

Or where we were headed.

Or why.

CHAPTER 2

"Ashley," I whispered to the robot. Somewhere, nearby or far away, my best friend was controlling this robot. "You can see all these soldiers, right?"

It was a dumb question. Of course she could see them. The robot transmitted visuals in all four directions through the video lenses perched on top of its body stem. What I was hoping for in Ashley's answer was something that made sense of all the action over the last few minutes.

Especially after endless hours of doing nothing since the arrest except staring at the ceiling and walls of my cell. No one had told me why my father and I were under arrest after our journey from Mars to Earth. No one had even talked to me; the food pushed into my cell came from a surly guard who ignored all my questions. And I'd had no idea what had happened to Ashley.

"Yes, I can see the soldiers, Tyce," she answered through the robot's speaker. "If you want, wave at them and smile. They're not going to hurt you. Soon enough, you'll find out why not. I can't say anything more. Not in front of them."

She'd spoken loud enough that the nearest soldiers

could overhear. I gave a weak smile. If they smiled in return, I couldn't tell. Not with the lights of the corridor bouncing off the mirrored visors of their helmets.

"Ashley?" I took comfort from knowing she was somewhere on the other end of the remote X-ray signals that the robot's computer converted to brain-wave signals. I pictured her big grin under the straight, dark hair she kept cut short. At 13, she was a year younger than me. Most of the time she seemed years smarter. Especially in math. "Ashley!"

"Hang on, Tyce," she answered. "I've got to concentrate on where we're going. I'm using my memory here, and I only saw the map once."

I knew exactly what she meant. Robot control took full concentration. Like her, whenever I handled my own robot, my eyes and ears were cut off from all sight and sound. That allowed me to pay full attention to the information delivered to me from the robot's eyes and ears. It would be no different for Ashley, wherever she was. She'd probably be wearing earplugs and some kind of blindfold. It meant, of course, she wouldn't be able to read a map on her end and still maintain control of the robot here.

"If it helps," I said, "it looks like the corridor ends ahead about 25 feet."

"Thanks." The robot continued its steady pace. "I do see it. If I remember, I need to turn left."

Thirty seconds later the robot turned to follow the left branch of the corridor.

The scenery didn't change much, or the bright lights. Every 10 feet there was another closed door on each side. The soldiers kept following, their neuron rifles still aimed at my head.

I could hear Ashley count aloud through the robot's voice. "One . . . two . . . three . . . four . . . five . . ."

I realized she was counting doors.

At the tenth door, Ashley stopped and spun the robot's wheels so that the robot was facing the door. With me still in its arms.

"Grab the handle," Ashley instructed. "I'd use the robot hands, but I'm afraid of dropping you."

"Sure." From the arms of the robot, I reached out for the handle. The robot held me steady. With the strength in its titanium arms, it could have effortlessly held a person five times my weight.

"Open the door," Ashley directed me. "It should be unlocked."

She was right. The door opened easily. The robot rolled through.

I gasped as the door shut behind us on its automatic hinges.

It was another prison cell. With two men sitting on the bunk. One man held a knife to the other's throat.

The man being held captive I didn't recognize. Wearing an outfit that looked like a one-piece cape, he was elderly and very small. His hair was white, and the wrinkles on his face were deep enough to hold water if he stepped outside in a rainstorm. A slightly worried frown rearranged those wrinkles.

The man holding the knife I did recognize. He was much younger, with square shoulders, a square face, and hair the same color of blond as mine. A big man, wearing a regulation military jumpsuit—like the ones I'd been given during the quarantine process.

This man shifted slightly where he sat on the edge of the bunk, without moving the knife from the older man's throat.

He had the older man carefully positioned as a shield, making it risky for the guards to try a neuron shot.

"Hello, Tyce," this man said calmly.

I knew the man holding the knife very well. I had just spent six months in space with him.

"Hello, Dad," I said, cradled helplessly as I was in the robot's arms. "How are you?"

CHAPTER 3

"As a result of this gentleman remaining here with me," Dad said to me, "the Combat Force commander here at this base has agreed to my conditions. Which includes freedom for you and Ashley."

Combat Force. The military arm of the World United Federation.

"He's going to remain with you?" I asked.

The old man did not react to what Dad said. Just sat there patiently, as if it were a regular happening to have someone hold a knife to his throat.

"Just me and Ashley are going?" I continued. I didn't know why we had been arrested. I only knew Ashley had been in another prison cell; Dad must have arranged to get her released first. "But what about—"

"Me? No, Tyce. Say nothing more."

By the tone of Dad's voice, I knew I had to obey.

"I wish we could talk freely," Dad continued, "but I have no doubt that this room is under audio surveillance. So don't say anything unless it is a direct reply to one of my questions. Got that?"

"Yes," I said, unfair as it seemed. I had plenty of my own questions that I desperately wanted to ask Dad.

Why had we been arrested?

Who was this man he held hostage?

How had Dad been able to get a knife?

What were we going to do about the armed soldiers out in the corridor?

"Tyce," Dad said, "you remember why you and Ashley came back to Earth?"

"Yes."

"When both of you leave here, you must do it. Even without me. Understand?"

Without him?

"Dad, I—"

"Answer me with a yes. You *will* do it without me. Understand?"

"Yes."

"As part of my conditions, you and Ashley will each be equipped with money cards. Don't be afraid to spend what you need because the cards have no limit. Get there and complete the mission. Understand?"

"Yes."

"You only have six days. If you succeed, you can return here for me."

Succeed at what? And if we don't succeed, what will happen to Dad?

"Now carefully reach into my chest pocket. Take the folded piece of paper there. I've written out all the rest of the things I can't say to you here in this cell."

From wherever she was, Ashley moved the robot slowly forward and stopped it just in front of my father.

Two days' worth of beard darkened Dad's face. Half circles of exhaustion showed under his eyes.

"Dad, you all right?" I asked.

He nodded briefly, his lips tight.

The top of the paper showed from his chest pocket. In the robot's arms, I leaned forward. As I did, the old man beside Dad grabbed my lower arm.

A sudden sharp pain stabbed my skin.

"Hey!" I yelled.

"Let him go," Dad warned, pressing the knife harder against the old man's throat. I expected to see blood. Instead, I noticed Dad was using the dull side of the knife.

The dull side?

It didn't make sense. But I was in no position to comment. Especially with the stabbing pain against the underside of my arm.

"Let him go," Dad said again, his voice growing more intense.

Weird. Dad's voice was louder as if he was angry, but I knew Dad well enough to know when he truly was mad. Who is Dad trying to fool?

Finally the old man released my arm.

I looked at my skin and saw blood.

How had the old man managed to break skin?

So many questions. And none that I can ask.

"Tyce," Dad ordered, "take the note. Time matters a great deal. When you read it, you'll understand why."

I ignored the tiny drops of blood on my arm, pulled the paper loose from Dad's chest pocket, and slipped it into my own pocket. The robot backed away, holding me safely.

"I have also arranged for you and Ashley to have a radio linked by satellite to a radio that will be provided to me," Dad said. "Use it to speak to me only when necessary. Remember, we need to keep our communications to a minimum, because I'm sure we will be monitored. Also remem-

ber it's important that you report to me every half hour."
Dad smiled grimly as he continued. "Without those reports,
this gentleman here is in serious trouble."

The old man's frown deepened.

"You are his lifeline," Dad explained to my puzzled look.
"As long as I know you are safe, he is safe. If they send anyone after you, if they stop you in any way—"

"No need to explain," the old man interrupted. He hadn't
said a word to this point, and the calm deepness of his voice
was a surprise. "If the kids get hurt, I get hurt. The Combat
Force commander knows this very clearly. All your conditions
have been met. But I warn you now, their deaths will be in
your hands."

"If anyone in the Combat Force harms them . . . ," Dad
began to say.

"It won't be the Force that kills them, you young fool."

I'd never heard anyone speak to my father this way.
More surprisingly, Dad accepted the rebuke.

Who is this old man?

"Sending them out into the swamps of the Everglades
will kill them as surely as any military command," the old
man continued.

Everglades?

"And furthermore, young man," he told Dad, "exactly
how long do you think you can stay awake?"

Dad didn't answer. At least not to the old man.

"Tyce," Dad replied, "he's right. All I can guarantee you
for a head start is the length of time that I can sit here.
When I fall asleep . . ."

He didn't have to finish that thought. I understood.
When Dad fell asleep and the knife fell from his hand, he'd
no longer have a hostage.

"I won't leave you," I blurted. "Send Ashley by herself.

I'll help you. We can take turns staying awake and keeping him hostage while she—"

"Go," Dad insisted. "Later, when you read the note, you'll understand." He gave me a look I couldn't interpret.

"No."

"Tyce," Dad said gently, "you'll have to trust me. I'm your father."

"No," I said. "I won't leave you."

"You have no choice."

Dad lifted his eyes from mine and stared directly into the front video lens of the robot that held me. "Ashley, take him away."

The robot began to roll back toward the door, with me still helpless in its arms.

"No!" I shouted at the robot. "Ashley, let me stay!"

My desperate plea did no good.

The prison door opened behind me.

My last view of my father was of him sitting on the bunk. With a solemn, sad expression on his face.

"You need to succeed, Tyce. You have six days. And the countdown begins now."

CHAPTER 4

With soldiers following, the robot approached the main doors of the Combat Force's prison.

I now knew why they had not fired any shots from their neuron rifles.

Dad was protecting me by holding that old man hostage. But only for as long as he could remain awake.

At that instant I hated like I'd never hated before. I hated the fact that I was being carried. I hated the fact that the operation on my spine had left me without the use of my legs. I hated the fact I couldn't get to my feet and charge back to the prison cell. That I couldn't help the father I used to dislike and had only recently come to understand. I couldn't lose him now—especially when he'd also become my friend.

But I was helpless. As the robot rolled forward I didn't even bother pleading with Ashley anymore. A few steps later I heard Mom's voice in my mind. *Tyce, we just have to trust God. Even when things look bad, he's got everything under control.* She'd said it before, and she'd been right. But what about this time? Although I, too, had come to believe in and trust God, this situation looked impossible. How was God going to fix this?

And now the doors to the outside loomed in front of me. Despite my anger and fear, I began to feel excitement. Like opening a present on Christmas, except a thousand times stronger.

It had been night when Dad, Ashley, and I and the rest of the crew of the *Moon Racer* had been shuttled from orbit to Earth. We had landed at this military base, and the shuttle had coasted into a large warehouse. On the ground we'd been transferred through a chute from the shuttle into an electric vehicle that took us deeper into the base. Finally we'd reached the prison area after a brief time in quarantine. Not once during the process had I seen anything of the Earth's surface. I had not even gulped one lungful of outside air.

And now?

When the doors in front of me opened, I'd be somewhere I had dreamed about for years. Ever since understanding that I was the only person in the entire solar system to be born off the planet Earth.

Yes, I'd be outside, without a space suit. On Earth. Breathing in open air, outside of buildings. For the first time in my life. As the main doors swung open to the outside, I sucked a big lungful of air and held my breath.

The next instant I lost all that air. For what I saw took my breath away.

Blue sky!

Yellow sun!

White clouds!

On Mars, the landscape revealed a butterscotch-colored sky with a blue sun and orange clouds. I'd only ever read or seen on DVD-gigarom disc how things looked on Earth. This was far more beautiful than I'd ever imagined.

In that moment, I forgot briefly about my dad. I forgot about the six-day countdown. I forgot about the impossible mission of rescue that Ashley and I faced.

Blue sky!

Yellow sun!

White clouds!

And heat. Wonderful warmth on my skin. With air moving across me.

I drew in another lungful of breath—just because it was so sweet to drink in this fresh air.

The ground was black and smooth in front of me. This was the end of the runway that the shuttle had landed on when we'd been taken here. A few different airplanes— which I recognized from movies I had watched on Mars— were parked at the side of this runway. To my left and to my right were all the buildings of the military base, including the large tall bay that the shuttle had parked in. All of this looked like an island set in the middle of the swamps that surrounded it.

As the robot rolled closer to the edge of the runway, I was overwhelmed by smells that came with the air I drank in so greedily. I was used to a landscape of frozen brown and red desert, long sucked dry of any hint of moisture. Here? Beyond the parking lot was a wall of green. Tall plants reaching for the sky! Small plants crowding the bases of the large plants. With colorful blossoms that gave incredible smells. Wow! Wow! *Wow!*

And noises! The creaking and buzzing and twittering of living things that swarmed in the green plants at the edge of the parking lot.

This was Earth!

How incredible.

"Tyce? Tyce?" Ashley's voice broke through.

"I can hear you," I finally answered.

"It's OK," she said. "Really, it's OK."

I didn't answer her. I was still trying to comprehend all of this. *This is really Earth!*

"We'll get through this," Ashley promised through the robot's speakers. "In less than a week, you'll see your dad again. We'll make sure of it."

I suddenly realized why she was trying to reassure me. Because I suddenly realized I was crying, and the sound of it must have reached her. She didn't know I wasn't crying because of my dad. But because of how beautiful God's creation was. *Earth!*

"Ashley," I stuttered, "I . . . I . . ."

I couldn't finish. I couldn't find any words to express what it felt like to be outside, under the blue sky of Earth, for the first time in my life. Instead, I turned my eyes to the sky and thought, *Wow, God. Thanks.*

"Hang on," Ashley said. "I'll have you with me right away. I'm here. At the edge of the runway. In this boat."

I noticed for the first time that the trees in front of me weren't a solid wall. In the gap, I saw a large boat. With what looked like a giant fan mounted on the back. At the front of it stood a single man, his hands on a steering wheel. At the back was a canvas roof propped by four poles, one in each corner.

"Airboat," Ashley said, reading the question in my mind. "For riding the top of the shallow water of the Everglades."

I remembered what the old man had said in Dad's prison cell. *Sending them out into the swamps of the Everglades will kill them as surely as any military command.*

We were going out there? Into all those trees and plants

and among all those strange noises of all that hidden, buzzing life? On water?

Suddenly the familiar, barren, frozen desert of the Martian landscape seemed like a very safe home.

CHAPTER 5

A heavy rumbling noise came from the boat's motor.

The robot rolled up a ramp onto the boat. Below the ramp was dark water that smelled strange to my accustomed-to-Mars nostrils.

Water! The boat rested in a channel hundreds of yards long that finally disappeared in the distance among the trees and vegetation.

Water! I could hardly comprehend so much water out in the open. On Mars, water was as precious as electricity and oxygen, and it was guarded and recycled as if our lives depended on it. Which, of course, they did.

Yet here was water, in the open, and more of it than I'd seen in my entire life. I might have stopped to stare with an open jaw, but the robot reached the top of the ramp and rolled into the boat.

The 20 soldiers with the neuron rifles remained at the edge of the parking lot until we had boarded. Then they lowered their rifles and turned to leave, walking in tight formation in their dark brown uniforms.

The soldier behind the wheel at the front of the boat wore an identical uniform and had the standard, clipped-short hair. His tan face showed no expression. Nor did he say anything.

I ignored him in return.

My attention was on Ashley.

She sat at the back of the boat, propped by seat cushions to stay upright, since her own body was basically helpless as she controlled the robot. She wore a blindfold and a headset. Around the waist of her military jumpsuit was a robot pack, which is a mini-transmitter. It was the "bot-pack" that made my rescue possible. All my life on Mars, I'd worked in a laboratory under the dome, hooked into a large computer system that was definitely not portable. When Ashley had arrived on Mars, she'd brought the next generation of robot-control technology—the bot-pack, a mobile robot-control package that hung on a belt.

"Welcome, Martian," the robot said to me.

Good old Ashley. Making a joke about my origins. "Hello, earthling," I fired back.

It was weird. Ashley was only a couple of steps away from me, under the shade of the canvas roof. Yet she wasn't seeing me with her eyes, but through the robot's video lenses. She didn't speak to me with her voice, but through the robot's speakers. Only after she disengaged from the robot would the reverse happen. The robot would become lifeless, and then Ashley would use her own body to see me and talk to me.

"Don't think being so friendly is going to help," I said. "That's my father you made me leave behind in there. I—"

"You need to get into your wheelchair," she interrupted. "It's an older model, but all they could come up with here on short notice. Once you're in it, you can yell at me all you want."

A wheelchair was parked beside Ashley. Not the one I'd

taken with me from Mars, but a bigger one, with an electric motor. Another full-size robot stood beside it. A bot-pack hung from the left handle of the wheelchair. A backpack hung from the other handle.

"No," I said stubbornly. "Once I get into the wheelchair, this boat will leave, won't it? And my father will be by himself."

"Tyce," Ashley reasoned through the robot's speakers, "in two more minutes when I get a chance to talk to you, all of this will be clear. Let me disengage from the robot, so I can explain to you what I know. Your dad's note will do the rest. But I don't want to treat you like a baby and force you into the wheelchair. Please?"

Finally I nodded.

The robot moved the extra few feet to the wheelchair and gently lowered me into place. The boat rocked in the water at the shifting of our weight.

"All right," I said, as the robot backed away. "I'm ready."

The robot parked itself beside the other robot. It lowered its arms. Shutters dropped to protect the video lenses. I knew what Ashley was doing because of the countless times I had done it myself. Disengaging from the robot controls by shouting *"Stop!"* in her mind.

A second later Ashley's hands moved upward as she pulled off her headset and blindfold. She blinked against the brightness of the sun and pushed back her straight, black hair. The sun highlighted her cheekbones, beautiful dark eyes, and Asian features. When Ashley grinned, she looked her age. But when she frowned, people stepped back. She appeared grown-up enough to be intimidating.

This time she neither grinned nor frowned but gave me a gentle smile. "Hey, Tyce. It's good to see you."

It was good to see her too. But I was still mad enough that I didn't want to say it. Before I could think of something else to say instead, she raised her voice and spoke to the soldier at the front of the boat.

"We're ready. Take us away."

The motor roared, the giant fan blades began to whir, and we shot forward in the water.

CHAPTER 6

In one way, Ashley was immediately wrong.

Despite her promise, she wasn't able to tell me much in the next two minutes. Not with the roar of the motor and the fan blades. Wind whipped my face and my hair, a sensation I loved. I had never felt anything like it.

The boat rocked and shook as it sped down the flat water of the channel. Ashley squatted beside me and moved her face close to my ear.

"Like I said before, most boats have propellers!" she shouted. "But that would never get us through the Everglades. We'll have to put up with the noise for a couple of hours!"

"Where are we going?"

"To the western edge of the Everglades! They've arranged for a helicopter to take us from there!"

"Why not just have the helicopter pick us up at the base!" I yelled back.

"Good question!" she answered. "I've wondered myself!"

"What if we get lost!" I shouted back. It had taken less than 30 seconds for the channel to take us deep into the thick vegetation. It was as if the Combat Force base no longer existed.

"GPS!" she shouted. "Global Positioning Satellite! Same as on Mars!"

I nodded. Satellites that orbited Mars fed signals to handheld global positioning units, making it possible to pinpoint your location on a grid of the planet.

The boat swung violently to make a turn. I clutched the arms of my wheelchair. I was glad someone had tied it to the side to keep it from rolling.

Ashley toppled over. When she recovered, she squatted beside me again. "I'm going to sit at the side of the boat! In the meantime, read your dad's note!"

Instead of shouting again, I simply nodded.

Ashley moved to the seat at the side of the boat.

I reached into my pocket, opened the note, and began to read.

Tyce, there is much that confuses me about all of this. What I can guess comes from the questions I was asked by Combat Force officials since we landed on Earth. It seems that although Dr. Jordan is high up in Combat Force command, no one in the World United Federation government or the Combat Force knew about Dr. Jordan's project with Ashley and the others. Evidently, as a secret agent for the rebel force Terratakers, he has run this project without authorization. Nor, somehow, does anyone know about the recent events on Mars, including the hostage taking under the dome or the Hammerhead testing. It's as if all communications from Mars to Earth over the last six months were silenced without the knowledge of anyone on Mars. My guess is that Luke Daab controlled all communications by computer, just as he did on the Moon Racer.

Dr. Jordan's last communication from the Moon Racer was that we had abandoned him in outer space to kill him. He wanted it to look like he was dead, and at the same time cast suspicion on us. That was the reason we were initially arrested.

I have said nothing about him surviving, simply because I didn't know if I could trust anybody, not until finally talking with the Supreme Governor. I'm now glad I said so little to the Combat Force people here.

Because of the robots on our ship and the other equipment, they are very curious about you and Ashley. Two of the highest generals in the Combat Force are scheduled to arrive this afternoon to oversee experiments on you and Ashley. It was imperative that you both escape before that happened. Once they understand what you are capable of doing, they will want to use you in the same ways that Dr. Jordan intended.

Also, you know Dr. Jordan ejected from the Moon Racer in an escape pod. At this point, he has no reason to think his plan to destroy the Moon Racer failed. As you also know, he has already arrived, but, as far as I can tell, he has kept this hidden from his Combat Force connections. It wasn't until meeting with the Supreme Governor that I learned what he has been doing since reaching Earth and what he intends.

This is the second reason you and Ashley needed to escape immediately. Once Jordan knows you are still alive, he will try to capture you, and failing that, send someone to kill you. I'm sure Jordan would prefer to see you dead than let the World United Federation truly understand the scope of his project. After all, he still has all the other kids under his control for as long as the Federation does not discover their existence.

No one on an official level in the Federation or the Combat Force knows about Dr. Jordan and the others except you and me and Ashley. When the generals arrive, I am sure they will ask me about you two, especially after Ashley demonstrated her control of a robot by rescuing you. They will not, however, have any reason to suspect there are others. Or that I know there are others.

You and Ashley, then, must keep their existence secret as you try to find a way to stop Dr. Jordan. Trust no one unless they prove I have sent them. You must also reach the other kids before Dr. Jordan or the Combat Force does. If possible, get them to a place where the media can report them. Once the world knows of them, they will no longer be considered a secret weapon. And they, along with you, will finally be safe. Once that happens, the Combat Force will have no reason to keep me prisoner.

If you don't have time to reach the media, you need to find a way to stop Dr. Jordan. I can't stress this enough. Stop him even if it means my death.

Also, immediately get rid of the radio. I only referred you to it for the sake of the listening device. It may have a tracking device. Don't worry about sending back reports. I have arranged another way to follow your progress. Nor do you need to worry about me. I have no intention of harming my hostage. In fact, I will be releasing him before the afternoon is over. In turn, he will make sure I come to no harm, at least for the next six days while you get proof for the world about Jordan's secret program. You see, this man is . . .

Dad's words reached the end of the front of the page. I stopped for a second, wondering about the last paragraph. For the sake of the listening device. How much had been said in there that I misunderstood? I sure hoped I was about to get the rest of the answers. I began to turn the page over to read the rest.

A sudden drop in noise, however, distracted me.

The boat's engine began to sputter, and the fan blades lost their power.

Just as suddenly, the engine quit and the sputtering ended completely.

Ashley darted forward beside me. I folded the note and put it back in my pocket.

What was going on?

The boat began to coast toward the edge of the channel. Blades of long grass slapped at the hull.

"The radio," I told Ashley. "Get on the radio and let Dad know what's happened."

He had told me to get rid of it, but I thought he'd at least want to know about this new development. After that, I'd throw it overboard.

"Sure," Ashley said. "I'll—"

Our pilot screamed and fell over. He lay, shaking out of control, on the floor of the boat. His feet thumped a wild drumming pattern.

Only one thing could have done that to him. A neuron rifle! But who and where . . .

Movement ahead answered my question.

A low, flat boat glided silently out of the vegetation, where it evidently had been waiting in ambush. A man stood at the front, holding with both hands a long pole that stuck into the ground beneath the water. He leaned into the pole, and the boat moved closer. He pulled it loose, lifted it, stuck it into the ground again, and leaned, repeating this quickly until he was almost at our own boat.

It was then that I saw the neuron rifle behind him, on the seat of the flat boat.

But only Combat Force soldiers are authorized to have neuron rifles, I thought wildly. *And even then, a neuron rifle doesn't work unless its internal computer chip reads a fingerprint pattern belonging to an authorized user.*

This man, in his tattered dark clothing, definitely did not look military. Nor did he look like an authorized user.

He grinned wildly, his teeth shining brightly beneath a

greasy wide-brimmed hat. He had a big, bushy black beard, and equally bushy long hair. A large knife was strapped on a belt around his waist.

"Come in!" Ashley shouted into the radio behind me. "Come in. We're under attack."

The other boat was much lower in the water than ours. The wild man stared upward into my eyes. He kept grinning.

"You can tell her the radio won't work." He took one hand off his pushing pole and pointed to a small black box beside the neuron rifle on the seat of the boat. "This little gadget jams any electrical signals for 100 yards in any direction. It's how I got your boat engine to quit. And it's why no one can hear your friend, no matter how loud she yells into her radio."

He grabbed a rope and put the end of it in his mouth. With clenched jaws and both hands free, he reached upward and took hold of the edge of our boat to pull himself in. With a grunt and a quickness that surprised me in a man so large, he rolled over the edge and landed feetfirst in our boat.

"Don't try anything stupid," he said as he spit out the rope in his mouth. The other end of the rope was tied to his flat-bottom boat. With quick movements of nimble fingers, he tied this end to our boat, securing both boats together. "Make this easy on me. And I promise you won't get hurt."

CHAPTER 7

The wild man took a short piece of rope out of his pocket and stepped toward Ashley. "Drop the radio," he said. "Give me your hands."

Ashley threw me the radio.

"Give me your hands," he repeated.

"No." Ashley kicked him in the shins.

He laughed. "Really," he said. "I don't want to hurt you. Let's get this over with."

She tried kicking him again, but he had reached out and placed his right palm on her forehead. She couldn't reach him, hard as she tried.

The laughter left his voice. "Young woman, there is no place for you to go. You wouldn't be able to swim 50 yards before a gator got you."

Gator?

"No, no, no," Ashley said. "If you really aren't going to hurt us, you wouldn't try to tie my hands."

"You're worth a lot of money if I deliver you safely, and that's what I intend to—" the wild man began. He had all but ignored me, assuming, I'm sure, that just because I was in a wheelchair I was useless. But as Ashley kicked at him, he backed up, almost to my legs.

In that second I threw the radio overboard. Then I pushed upward off the handles of my wheelchair and managed to wrap my arms around his neck.

The wild man grunted again, this time with surprise. He clawed at my arms, trying to pull me free.

I had no muscle control over my legs, but since I'd spent a lifetime using my arms to push my wheelchair around, I had far more strength in my upper body than most people guessed. Big and strong as this wild man was, he wasn't able to shake me loose.

He began to thrash around as I choked the air from his windpipe. I just wanted him unconscious. Ashley began to punch him in the stomach.

"Aaarrgh!" He thrashed harder, then moved to the side of the boat. Before I could react, he spun around so that I was hanging from his neck and shoulders above the water. "Aaarrgh!"

He was fading. I could tell by the way his attempts to yank my arms loose got weaker and weaker. But if he fell backward . . .

And that's exactly what happened. My weight pulled him toward the water, and he toppled out of the boat. With me clinging to his neck. Together we fell into the side of the flat-bottom boat.

There was a horrible thunk as his head slammed into the wood, and in the next instant, we hit water.

In shock, I let go. I gasped and water choked me. Panicked, I splashed frantically with my arms. The most water that had ever surrounded me was the fine spray of a shower on Mars. I had no idea how to swim and yet, somehow, my splashing kept my head above water. My eyes cleared, and I saw the side of the flat-bottom boat above me. I jabbed one hand upward, and my fingers closed on the edge. It gave me enough leverage to pull up with the other hand.

The flat-bottom boat tilted toward me as I clung to the side. The neuron rifle and black box slid toward me.

With my body weight supported by the water, I was able to pull halfway out. But that was it. I couldn't get any more of my body into the boat.

"Tyce!" Ashley shouted. "Tyce! Help me roll him over."

Out of the corner of my eye, I saw a flash. Ashley had used the boat hook to reach down for us. Holding to the side of the boat, my legs dangling uselessly in the water, I turned my head.

Ashley had managed to get the hook into the wild man's clothing. But he floated facedown. Blood streamed into the water from where he'd hit his skull.

Clinging to the flat-bottom boat with one arm, I reached for the wild man with the other. I grabbed a limp arm and rolled him over. Ashley worked the hook loose and then hooked his belt to support most of his weight. With one hand I held his head above the water. With the other arm I clung to the boat.

"I'm not sure how long I can hold him," I groaned. With his weight dragging on me, my armpit was already numb.

I looked up at Ashley. She stood at the side of the boat, leaning over, holding the boat-hook pole with both hands as she kept the wild man from sinking. Her eyes were focused beyond me, however, and her jaw had opened in shock.

"Hold him, Tyce," she shouted. "Just for a couple of seconds."

She disappeared from view. I couldn't turn my head to see what she'd seen. Without the support of her boat hook, the wild man's weight doubled. I nearly collapsed, and the flat-bottom boat tilted even more dangerously toward us.

A second later she was back, with the wild man's neuron rifle. She pointed it beyond me and the boat.

"What is it?!" I shouted.

"You don't want to know!"

I saw her trigger finger pull several times.

"What is it!" I shouted again. "The rifle isn't programmed for you! It won't shoot!"

"Alligator," she shouted back. "And it's headed right for the both of you!"

CHAPTER 8

Alligator!

I'd seen them, but only on the DVD-gigaroms on computer screens. Growing up on Mars, I'd spent endless hours learning everything I could about Earth. Earth animals fascinated me, and some of my favorite clips had been of the giant predators. Lions, tigers, sharks. And, of course, alligators.

My mouth instantly went dry with fear.

Alligator! I knew it didn't bite its prey to death. No, it pulled the prey underwater—a person, deer, anything too large to swallow—and spun it underwater in circles until it drowned. Then it found an underwater log and jammed the dead prey into place until it had rotted soft enough to tear apart.

I didn't want that prey to be me.

Frantically, I turned my head, straining until it felt like my neck would snap.

And I saw it.

Like a giant log, but with an evil, narrowing snout, it approached slowly. It was probably drawn by the sound of our thrashing in the water, or maybe by the smell of the wild man's blood. Its eyes were barely above the water. Its tail twisted the surface of the water with powerful, snakelike thrusts.

Alligator!

"Ashley," I gasped. "Jump into the lower boat!"

She understood immediately. That was our only chance. That she stand in the flat boat and haul us in from there.

When she landed, the flat-bottom boat swayed dangerously, but it was low enough and wide enough to give the stability she needed.

She grabbed my shoulder and began to pull me upward.

The wild man was still unconscious.

"No," I said. "Him first."

Ashley grabbed him by the hair, bringing him close enough to grab his shoulders. She leaned way back in the boat to get her weight on the far side. With my free hand I held his shirt and pushed upward.

He was too heavy. It wasn't going to work.

I twisted my head. The gator was about 10 seconds away!

"Try harder!" I shouted.

The wild man coughed and sputtered. His eyes opened wide. For a split second, I stared into his startlingly blue eyes.

"Gator!" I shouted at him. "Get in!"

He looked past me and saw the gator.

Seven seconds away.

He grabbed the side of the boat. Then, with his other hand, he grabbed the back of my jumpsuit. With a heave of his other huge arm, he flung me upward and over the edge of the boat.

I landed hard with my chin on the seat of the boat. Stunned. Water streamed from my jumpsuit.

I pushed up on my arms. My face bumped into the little black box that he had used to jam the electrical signals.

The gator was almost on the wild man.

His hand came out of the water with his knife. He lifted it high.

The gator's mouth opened wide, showing yellow, jagged teeth and the pink, soft inside of its throat.

And as the thought entered my mind, I acted.

I picked up the little black box and fired it into that wide-open mouth.

The jaws snapped shut.

The gator roared! It flipped over and thrashed wildly, side to side.

The wild man screamed at the same time. He began to sink in the water. Ashley grabbed his arm and held him to the side of the boat.

She, too, screamed.

Then it was over. The gator sank. And Ashley and the wild man gasped for breath.

"You felt that too?" he said to Ashley.

She nodded. "A shock when I touched you."

"Trust me," he said, recovering his breath. "It was worse on me. I was in the water. And it's a great conductor of electricity." His massive chest heaved against the fabric of his wet shirt. Then, out of the blue, he began to laugh. "If electricity from the black box was shocking you and me, think of what it was doing to that gator." He wiped blood from his forehead. Water dripped from his matted beard. The wild man directed his next words at me. "When that gator was coming, you could have got into the boat first."

"Maybe," I answered. I felt dumb lying stomach-first in the boat with my head resting on the seat and peering upward like some baby crawling on the floor. So I pulled myself up by my arms and rolled over to a sitting position. My jumpsuit was squishy with water. A few strands of green weed clung to my chest. "But I would have had to let go of you first. I was afraid you'd sink."

"Which means you saved my life." The wild man shook his head. Blood kept dribbling down into his eyebrows. He must have had a cut hidden somewhere under his thick hair. "Actually, twice. Because you zapped the gator with the black box. I'm not sure my knife would have done much good against that monster."

He grinned, and his teeth flashed white against his dark, wet beard. "I guess I owe you then. That changes things so completely that I don't have much choice but to go on the run. With you." He shook his head and grinned wryly. "Plus you just cost me a million dollars."

"Pardon me?"

"I'll explain later. We've got less than five minutes to clear this area. Or all of us are dead."

As if in answer to him, we heard the roar of boat motors in the distance.

He got to his feet. The flat-bottom boat wobbled as he stepped toward our bigger boat and hauled himself into it. Moving quickly to the front, the wild man lifted the unconscious pilot and dragged him to the edge above us.

"Sounds like them," he said. "Help me get this guy down into the flat-bottom. Because now I'd say we have less than two minutes."

CHAPTER 9

"My name is Nate!" he shouted above the noise of the engine. "Guys in the platoon called me Wild Man. Ashley and Tyce, right?"

With effortless efficiency, he had already lifted Ashley up from the flat-bottom boat into our boat. He'd done the same with me, setting me into my wheelchair as if gravity didn't exist for us.

Next he'd moved forward and restarted the engine.

"Right!" Ashley answered.

She gave me a strange look. I could guess what she was thinking. *How does he know our names?*

I expected Nate to get us out of here immediately.

Instead, he knelt by the dash of the boat and reached underneath. When he pulled his hand back, I saw a small gray box, with some wires dangling from where he had ripped it loose.

"Tracking device!" Nate shouted. "Now they'll have to find us the old-fashioned way!"

Tracking device? How could he know about that too?

Nate threw the tracking device into the flat-bottom boat,

where the pilot was just beginning to wake up from the neuron blast.

"Adios!" he shouted at the pilot.

Nate slammed the controls into forward, and the boat shot ahead into the channel.

He knew our names. He knew about the hidden tracking device. He'd known where to wait in ambush. He'd been supplied a neuron rifle by someone from the Federation's Combat Force.

Was there an explanation for this on the back of Dad's note to me?

I had a sudden sick feeling.

The note! The note in my pocket!

I'd fallen into the water. What would be left of the note?

The boat lurched. I managed to snap open my chest pocket. All I was able to extract was a soggy wad of useless paper.

What had I missed? What had been on the other side of the note to guide Ashley and me?

I leaned back in my wheelchair, angry and frustrated.

Nate maneuvered the boat at top speed, throwing Ashley and me from side to side as we followed the twists of the channel farther and farther into the swamp.

Then I watched with horror as he gunned the boat to even higher speeds on the next straight stretch.

Ahead was a turn, but there was no way we'd make it at this speed.

The boat charged forward, directly toward a wall of trees and high swamp grass!

Impact in less than three seconds!

Two!

One!

Bang! The front of the boat hit the shallow bank of land.

The impact threw me back in the wheelchair. If the brakes hadn't been set and if the wheelchair hadn't been tied in place, the force would have thrown the wheelchair out the back of the boat.

We were airborne!

I clenched my jaws, waiting for a bigger bang as the boat slammed into solid ground.

The boat motor still roared as the seconds seemed to stretch into a lifetime.

Splash! Nate had found a large open area of water on the other side of the land, screened by the vegetation, with a new channel visible at the far end.

Briefly Nate turned back to us from the steering wheel at the front of the boat. "That should lose them!" he shouted. "So settle back and enjoy the ride. We've got about another two hours ahead of us."

I couldn't help the thought that flashed through my mind.

And then what?

CHAPTER 10

The three of us sat in front of a small fire on a small island. The grass was packed down to make sitting more comfortable for Nate and Ashley. (The good thing about being in a wheelchair is that you always have a place to sit.) There were a few large trees with roots visible above the ground, so that it looked like they were resting on giant claws.

Three hours had passed since we had left the pilot behind in the flat-bottom boat. Two and a half of those hours we'd spent twisting and turning through the Everglades. Sometimes on open water, sometimes through channels, and often it seemed we were riding tall grass as the boat skimmed in shallow water.

It had been an incredible two and a half hours for me. The first part of the ride my mind had been full of questions chasing questions. When I'd finally realized that I had no hope of answering those questions without more information, I'd forced myself to think of other things. Like the sky and the wind and the smells and the sights.

For the rest of the boat ride, I had simply stared around me in amazement, trying to match what I saw in the Everglades with what I remembered from the DVD-gigaroms

I had watched all my life on Mars. The boat startled large white birds with long, skinny legs, sending them clumsily into the air. I saw turtles sunning on logs. Dozens of kinds of tiny colorful birds. Trees that were draped with long, dark moss, so that they looked like hunched-over old women.

Again and again I marveled at the new sights and smells. When Nate finally stopped the boat and cut the engine, I was able to hear bird cries and insects buzzing and the splash of fish jumping.

Amazing, I told myself again and again. *How could anyone live in all this and not believe someone created it?* But then again, it wasn't that long ago that I hadn't believed God had existed. It had taken a lot of crises at the dome to show me that God not only existed, but that he created the universe and cared about everything and everyone in it.

Just amazing, I thought, awed. I envied all the people who had grown up on Earth—which meant everyone in the solar system except for me—because they were able to see stuff like this every day of their lives.

I had mentioned how cool I thought Earth was—and everything on it—to Nate when he first helped me out of the boat and set me up in the wheelchair on dry land. He'd given me a strange look, followed by a smile. He said he would be happy to discuss that later but needed to get us supper first.

Then he had disappeared for 15 minutes, returning with three fish, each a little bigger than one of his large hands.

As he started a fire, I watched a tiny insect with wings land on the inside of my arm, just above the place where the old man had jabbed me and left a small scab of drying blood. The insect seemed so delicate, I marveled that it could fly.

I felt a tiny pinprick. Had this tiny thing actually bit me? I kept watching the insect. It began to swell.

"What are you doing?" Nate the wild man asked me. "Slap it. It's sucking your blood."

"Acck!" I slapped it. Blood spread across my arm.

"What planet are you from?" he joked. "Haven't you seen a mosquito before?"

So that's what it was. I'd read about them. I sure wasn't going to tell this man why I didn't know what it was. Dad's note had urged strict secrecy. From everyone.

Nate threw me a tiny can. "Spray this repellent on yourself. As the sun sets, they'll come out in droves."

"Thanks," I said.

"Thank me by trading with me," he answered.

"Trading?" Ashley echoed. "What do Tyce and I have that we can trade?"

"We'll trade information." Nate knelt beside the fish he had dropped on the grass. "You tell me things. I tell you things. Simple, right?"

He yanked loose his huge knife from his belt.

"Easy for you to say when you've got the knife," I told him. "Plus, you're easily 30 years old. I'm only 14 and in a wheelchair. At this point I'd be dumb to disagree with you."

Nate laughed. "Thirty-two. Which has nothing to do with this knife. Because you don't understand. The way I was raised, a man pays his debts. You saved my life twice. From here on I'm your protection. And from what little I can figure, you're going to need it."

He picked up one of the fish and held it upside down. With a quick movement, he slit the fish's belly from the tail to its gills. He reached into the fish and pulled out a long, stringy clump of gleaming colored tubes.

"What's that?" I asked. I was torn between two curiosities. What he'd meant by what he said. And what I was see-ing.

"Fish guts," he said. "How can you be as old as you are and not know that?"

He must not know I've grown up on Mars, I thought.

Ashley poked the guts with her finger. "Hmm." Ashley had spent a lot of her life in a secret institute. Evidently this was new to her too. She sniffed her finger and made a face.

It took less than a minute for Nate to take the guts out of the other fish too. He left the guts in a neat pile beside him. "Dinnertime," he announced.

"People eat fish guts?" I asked, startled. I could smell them from where I sat. I didn't know if I was that hungry just yet.

Another strange look from Nate. "Where *exactly* are you from? Mars or something?" He chuckled, then punched me in the shoulder.

I shrugged as an answer. I doubted he'd believe me any-way.

"I save those to use as bait to catch a turtle or two," Nate said to my shrug. "Turtle soup tastes great. And you can boil and eat it right out of its shell. God's made it an animal that provides its own bowl."

Nate rose and rinsed the gutted fish in the water beside us. He stopped at a bush and cut loose a green branch.

"See," he said, "this is our frying pan."

He poked the branch through one of the fish and held it above the fire.

"Now," he continued, "while these fish cook, let's talk."

CHAPTER 11

"I've got some questions, then," I said. The smell of the roasting fish made my mouth water. I wondered what "real food" would taste like. That was the kind of thing you could never experience on DVD-gigarom. Sure, I'd had a few meals in the prison. But they had been pretty tasteless, just like the nutrient-tubes I'd had all my life on Mars. The only difference was that the prison meals had been served on a tin plate rather than in a tube.

"I'll give you what answers I can," Nate replied. The fire popped and sent ashes and sparks upward, hitting him in the chest. He absently wiped the ash off. I now understood why his clothes smelled the way they did—wild and smoky.

"You had a neuron rifle programmed to allow you to shoot our pilot. I don't think you're a soldier. Even if you somehow stole or found the rifle, it takes a Combat Force computer to program it for you. Which means someone high up arranged it for you. So I'd like to know who gave you the rifle."

I stopped long enough to try the fish. Nate had instructed me to peel the meat back from the skin so that I wouldn't eat any scales. As promised, the white meat fell from the bones. With hesitation, I placed some in my mouth.

Wow! I'd never tasted anything so good in my entire life on Mars!

Nate smiled at my reaction. "More questions?"

I nodded but ate all my fish first, then licked my fingers clean.

"All right," I said. "How did you know our names? How did you know there was a tracking device on board and where it was? How did you know we were going to be coming down that channel at that time? How did you get the little black box to jam the electrical currents?"

Ashley jumped in. "And you knew that there would be boats chasing us. How? How did you know where to escape? And what did you mean when you said Tyce cost you a million dollars? And that now all three of us would be on the run?"

"And," I added, "you said you guessed we needed protection. What made you guess that?"

"You mean aside from the obvious?" he responded, grinning. "That you've escaped a Combat Force prison on the space base?"

"How could you even know that?" Ashley asked him. "Unless someone told you ahead of time. So who was that?"

"Even if someone didn't tell me," Nate returned, "there are the prison uniforms that are too large for each of you. Before you fall asleep tonight, I'll give you the clothes I got for you. You can change, and we'll burn the prison outfits."

"So you did know ahead of time," Ashley said.

"Yup." Nate took his knife out of his sheath again. I hoped he meant what he said about protecting us.

He slid the knife under the fish on the branch. With the

fish balanced on the blade, he handed it to Ashley. "Eat carefully," he said. "I'd hate to see you burn your fingers or your tongue."

Nate propped the next fish on a branch so that it would begin to cook. Ashley prayed quietly before she ate.

"I never used to do that myself," he said, waiting respectfully until she finished before he spoke. "But after a few years here in the swamps, I began to understand a lot more about God. And why, truly, we should thank him for what he gives us each day. I chose to believe in him, rather than ignore him as I used to. I just couldn't get away from the beauty of his creation that proves his very existence."

A few years in the swamps? No wonder it seemed like he was as comfortable living in the dangerous wildness of the Everglades as I had been living under the dome on Mars.

"I'll get to your questions first," he said next. "And most all of them are answered by telling you how I knew you'd be on this swamp boat on that channel when you were. But my answer is going to lead to my own questions, so be ready to return the favor."

I wasn't going to make promises, so I kept my mouth shut. Ashley was too busy eating to speak.

"As you might guess," Nate said, "I live here in the Everglades. About five years ago, I retired from the Combat Force. I was so tired of the fighting and the politics and the way the world was going that I decided I was done with it. So I ran—as far away from everything as I could. This natural preserve was as far away and wild as I could get."

Ashley spit some fish bones out, then smiled an apology at me.

"Yesterday, at the cabin I'd built 50 miles from the nearest road, my former commander dropped in on me.

Literally. By helicopter. Turns out I hadn't hidden myself as well as I thought. But then I was a fool to believe they wouldn't keep track of me. Not after the kinds of jobs I'd been given during my military service. I used to be part of an elite commando group. We'd be sent into places when the government wanted a problem solved quickly and quietly. . . ."

His voice trailed off and he stared into the fire.

It didn't seem like the kind of silence to interrupt.

I gazed above him, at the late-afternoon sky. The smudged clouds glowed with pinks, reds, and purples as the setting sun bounced light off them.

"Cannon—"

Ashley interrupted. "Cannon?"

"My former commander," Nate explained. "I was part of an elite platoon of the Combat Force. Called the E.A.G.L.E.S."

"Eagles?" I asked. "You flew?"

"E.A.G.L.E.S. I won't even try to explain what it stands for. In short, we were trained to fly anything, pilot any kind of boat, drive any vehicle. We were experts in things that now give me nightmares. Everything. Cannon is no longer in the E.A.G.L.E.S. platoon. He's now one of the top-ranking generals in the Combat Force. Imagine my surprise when he offered me a million dollars and the guaranteed privacy of a new identity for the rest of my life to help him with one last simple job. It didn't seem smart to turn him down. Not when it was obvious he could find me whenever he wanted."

"The simple job was to get us," I said.

"Yup, again. He told me who you were and gave me descriptions and some clothes he promised would fit. He told me that you would be released from prison because of a hostage taking. He provided me with the neuron rifle, the black box, and the time and location to wait in ambush. He warned me about the tracking device on the swamp boat. And he told me that once I stopped the swamp boat, because of the tracking device, there would be very little time before more soldiers from the prison began pursuit."

Nate paused. "I wasn't really doing it for the money. More to be left alone. He promised me he didn't mean you any harm, and I decided to take his word for it. I think I decided to believe him to make it easier on me. But I was just fooling myself. I mean, why does someone like him want to go to all the trouble to kidnap you guys?"

I could guess. It had something to do with robot control. But that wasn't something I wanted Nate to know.

"So instead of bringing you to him for whatever reasons he had in mind, I'm now promising to keep you away from him. That might answer all your questions. But only lead to more."

"Like how did the general know all of this?" Ashley said. "And what does he want with us?"

"You said he showed up yesterday," I added. "It wasn't until today that my dad got us out."

Ashley nodded. "Tyce, it was only a half hour before you got out of your cell that I was called down and released. How could anyone have known a full day earlier all of this was going to happen?"

I still didn't even know who my dad had taken hostage and how he'd managed to do it. I wished I hadn't ruined Dad's note by falling in the water.

"Tyce?" Ashley prompted me.

I sure wasn't going to let Nate know what Ashley and I needed to do. Dad had stressed the importance of keeping it secret. Even though Nate was now helping us, it still didn't seem smart to trust him. Not until I knew how much of what he told us was the truth.

I found my voice. "I guess when we know who sent the general, we'll have all the answers."

"Not *all* the answers," Nate corrected me. "Because now you owe me some. Who are you two, that my commander wants you so badly? And what's with the stuff in the boat? Those robot contraptions? And why were you taken to this high-secrecy Combat Force prison in the Everglades?"

"Ashley," I said, "Dad told me we had some money cards. Did you imprint them?"

"Yes. At least mine. Yours was already imprinted. I think they used a thumbprint from a cup you had handled in prison."

That was good.

Although I'd never used a money card on Mars, I knew how they worked. There was a special hologram place on the card that would hold only one thumbprint. Computers at banks, money machines, or store cash registers compared the thumbprint of the card with the thumbprint of the person with the card. If both prints matched, the transaction went through. If they didn't match, the reading machine immediately destroyed the card. This meant Ashley and I were safe from Nate. He couldn't just take our money cards and get rid of us. He needed Ashley and me to get the money.

"You're not answering my questions," Nate said firmly.

"I'd like to trade you something else instead," I answered. After all, Dad had said we had unlimited use of the money cards.

"What's that?"

As the darkness fell upon us, I gave Nate my best smile

as I made my offer. "How much money will it take for you to help us get where we need to go?"

"Where would that be?"

I coughed. "Ashley?"

She gave Nate a weak grin. "We, uh, can't tell you. Yet."

CHAPTER 12

Nate stared at the campfire. Ashley had fallen asleep in her sleeping bag. I sat to the side in my wheelchair.

I couldn't sleep. My arm itched, and there was a big lump on the surface of my skin. Nate told me it must be from the mosquito bite. I told him the mosquito had bitten me higher on my arm than that. When he laughed at me, I didn't bother going into detail how that old man in the prison had jabbed my arm.

I watched the fire flicker beyond my toes. Nate had made sure to keep the fire as small as possible so it couldn't be spotted by military pursuers. Suddenly, surrounded by the hum of mosquitoes, I felt lonely and afraid. It was a different kind of fear than I'd felt when all those crises had happened under the dome on Mars—the oxygen leak, the hostile takeover of the dome, and when Dad, Director Rawling, and I had almost been blown up by a black box under our platform buggy. I'd been on Mars—a world I knew well—then. Now I was on Earth, an alien place for me. Dad was in a military prison. And Mom and Rawling, the only other two adults I could count on, were 50 million miles away.

Yet, now there was so much for Ashley and me to do. She'd spent most of her life in something she called the "Institute," where she'd received her robot training along with 23 other kids her age. She'd only been able to tell Dad and me a few things about it during the trip from Mars to Earth, and we had intended to wait for a secure Internet link to try to use those clues. But would that be enough for us to find it?

I wanted to start keyboarding my thoughts.

Starting tomorrow, we only have five days left of our countdown. Even if we find out where the Institute is, will that be enough time to reach it?

And even if we find the place in time, what then? How can we even get in, if it's surrounded by guards? How exactly are we supposed to go about exposing it to the world through the media?

And what if we can't trust Nate? What will happen to Dad if we fail?

On Mars, I'd learned the habit of keeping a diary. I'd found it helped me sort my thoughts. I had the comp-board with me, and it was tempting to add to my diary now. Especially because I could analyze all the angles once they were written down. But I didn't want Nate to be tempted to take the comp-board from me and read the diary to learn more about Ashley and me. He already knew we were worth big bucks if he delivered us to his former commander. If he found out how much more we were worth as experimental technology, he might decide to change his mind about helping us.

Without a way to get my thoughts down in my diary, it felt like my head was filled with rolling marbles.

I sighed and looked up at the stars.

They didn't look as clear from Earth as from Mars.

Logically I knew why, of course. The Earth's atmosphere distorted the light waves. But logic didn't take away my sense of awe at the beauty of the stars as they seemed to twinkle.

I thought of all I had seen on my first day on Earth outside the prison. How incredible it was to see everything that lived out in the open. On Mars, nothing lived outside of the dome. Without that little man-made bubble of air and moisture for protection, life couldn't exist. But here on Earth . . .

"Kid?" Nate said, appearing concerned. "You all right?"

"Sure," I said, hiding my worries.

"You want to tell me about all this gear you have? Those things look like robots and . . ."

"Robots?" I forced myself to laugh. "You don't see any equipment to run them, do you?"

It made me glad I hadn't made him curious about any information in my comp-board. Before Nate could say anything else, a loud groaning roar echoed from out of the darkness. "Relax," Nate said. The fire's tiny glow must have been enough light for him to see me flinch. "Male gator. Letting the world know he's here."

"Oh."

"He'll mind his own business," said Nate. "We're fine here."

"Oh."

"You're interesting to watch." Nate chuckled. "You look around as if the world is one giant candy store. And I agree, it's unbelievably amazing. But because most people see it every day, they take it for granted. Living in the swamp, I had to learn all over again how incredible the process of life and ecology is. And who created it all in the first place."

I almost blurted out that I had never seen it before. Even

so, it seemed difficult to think that people would take all of this for granted.

" 'O Lord, what a variety of things you have made! In wisdom you have made them all,' " said Nate in a poetic voice.

My jaw fell open. This was coming from Wild Man?

"'The earth is full of your creatures,' " he continued. "'Here is the ocean, vast and wide, teeming with life of every kind, both great and small. . . . Every one of these depends on you to give them their food as they need it. When you supply it, they gather it. You open your hand to feed them, and they are satisfied.' "

Nate grinned. "From Psalm 104. When you travel light like I do, you don't want to be burdened by a lot of books. So the Bible is the only book I carry. Even those who want to ignore God's existence will agree that the Bible is a collection of the greatest and most powerful writing produced in human history. More important, it's the story of God's relationship with us, and how we can come to know him personally. It took me a long time to figure that out." He paused, and a pained look crossed his face. "I wish I would have figured it out earlier. . . . As I said before, living in these swamps has made a lot of things clear to me, including my relationship with God. Seeing his world, I now know it takes more faith to disbelieve his existence than it takes to believe in him."

I nodded. I, too, had come to understand that there's more to life than what a person can see or hear or touch. That the only way to peace was a relationship with God.

I wanted to be able to trust Nate completely, and this helped. But as my mom had pointed out, a lot of people could talk the talk. You had to wait until they walked the walk to see if their faith meant as much to them as they claimed. And Dad had said to trust no one. So I just listened.

"Anyway," he said, shrugging, "I've spent enough time alone that I got into the habit of memorizing things from the Bible. I like to be able to recall verses at any time."

I finally asked one of the questions that had been bugging me. "Why did you decide to live alone in the swamp?"

"Tell you what," Nate said, grinning. "I'll tell you where I came from if you tell me where you came from."

"Can't," I said after a few seconds.

"Wish you could," he said, "but you're old enough to decide who you can trust."

The alligator in the nearby swamp roared again. A few minutes of silence passed.

"Good night, kid from nowhere," Wild Man finally said.

I did feel like a kid from nowhere. Like an alien on Earth. In a wheelchair, when most people could walk. With a spinal plug that made me even more of a freak. I knew Nate had been joking when he called me that, but it still hit too close to the truth. I didn't answer him.

He must have felt my coldness in the silence between us, but he spoke kindly. "You already told me you don't need help getting into your sleeping bag. So I'll wake you in plenty of time tomorrow morning."

He crawled into his own sleeping bag.

And left me alone in my wheelchair, staring at the fire, feeling very alone.

CHAPTER 13

The smell of the fire woke me up just before dawn. Along with another interesting smell.

"Eat quickly," Nate said from where he was crouched beside the fire on our miniature island in the middle of the Everglades. "We've got about two hours to reach our meeting point."

I was still in my sleeping bag. The night before Nate had given me a pair of blue pants. He called them jeans. I also wore a T-shirt and a sweater.

I let Nate help me out of the sleeping bag into my wheelchair, impressed all over again at how powerful he was.

Nate went back to the fire, then handed me a green bowl filled with brown liquid. I wasn't familiar with the smooth hard material. *Plastic?*

He grinned at the puzzlement on my face. "Turtle soup. Remember? Slurp it right from the shell."

I nodded and took a taste. A strange texture and rather drippy. But not bad. Nate's version of Earth food was much better than the nute-tubes on Mars.

Nate noticed Ashley had awakened as well. He handed her a bowl. She ate it from her sleeping bag.

"Hmmm," she said, after a slurp.

"Finish it quick and get ready to go," he told her. "The sooner we leave, the sooner we arrive."

"Where?" I asked. The sky was getting brighter, and I shivered in my sleeping bag in the predawn cold. Already the sounds of birds filled the air. As if they were happy to be alive. I couldn't blame them. Earth was fascinating.

"It's no coincidence that I chose this route away from the base," Nate put in. "It was the direction that put us closest to the interstate. I've got a friend who handles a mag-strip truck on the north-south route. He usually brings me supplies once every two weeks, and I meet him at a truck stop on the highway on the outer limits of the Everglades. After my ex-commander showed up the other day, I called this friend and set up a meeting with him for today. Just in case I needed to get away from this area quickly."

No coincidence? It seemed like too much of a coincidence. I was immediately suspicious. "How did you know you'd need him?"

Nate smiled grimly. "When I was running operations, I always set up a fallback plan in case anything went wrong. The way it looks now, not only is my ex-commander going to be looking for me after not showing up with you two, but so are the Combat Force people we escaped yesterday. To me, this definitely qualifies as something going wrong."

A little under two hours later, Nate let the swamp boat glide to a stop at the edge of some trees.

As the motor died, I heard a strange whooshing rumble on the other side of the trees. The thick green underbrush, however, did not let me see more than 10 feet, so I couldn't tell what was making the noise.

"He'll have parked his trailer as close to the path as possible," Nate said as he jumped from the boat and tied the rope to a tree. "That's how he does it when he delivers my supplies. So I'll make a couple of trips. I'll bring up our equipment first, then come back for you guys."

"Um, sure," I said. We didn't have much choice except to trust him. The alternative was to try to move by ourselves, which would be next to impossible. For two reasons. I was in my wheelchair. And Ashley and I didn't really know where we were going. Yet.

Nate jumped back on the swamp boat and rolled each robot forward. He jumped off the boat and reached up for the upper body of the first titanium robot. He tilted it forward across his shoulder.

"At least these things are light enough to carry. But they're going to be a pain to travel with," he said. "But I have a feeling they're the reason I was offered so much money for you. Sure you don't want to tell me about them?"

I shook my head. As did Ashley.

"Remember," I said. Ashley and I had talked with him earlier about our money cards and the unlimited funds. We weren't in danger that he'd steal them from us, because he didn't have the identity prints to use them. "When you get us where we need to go, you will get your million."

He grinned. "I remember. Of course, you still haven't told me where you need to go."

We didn't know yet. But this wasn't something I wanted to tell him.

With the robot over his shoulder, Nate turned and disappeared up the path. Thirty seconds later he reappeared and did the same with the second robot. He came back for a duffel bag with his own supplies. Then for me and Ashley.

To get me off the boat, he first lifted me and then set me

on the ground. Next he went back for my wheelchair before setting me in it and rolling me forward on the path toward the rumbling noises.

Ashley followed, carrying our gear.

When we reached the end of the path, one row of trees screened us from what lay beyond. Both robots and Nate's duffel bag sat nearby.

Finally I saw the source of the rumbling noise.

"Trucks!" I said in triumph, recognizing them from the DVD-gigaroms. There was a parking lot filled with huge trucks and trailers. And on the other side was a highway, with vehicles rumbling down the pavement at high speeds. I never would have guessed they'd be so big.

"You sound like you've never seen a truck before." Nate again eyeballed me.

I didn't answer. It was crucial to keep as many secrets for as long as possible.

Ahead of us, a truck had backed up to the edge of the parking lot. The back trailer doors were open. That, I guessed, was our destination. A truck stop. As Nate had explained, it was a rest area off the interstate where trucks fueled.

There were probably 50 trucks, so I wasn't too worried that we would be noticed. Until I saw the Combat Force soldiers. Guarding trucks with Federation colors.

Would they see us as we loaded our stuff onto the truck?

Before I could say anything to Ashley, there was a loud explosion.

And the front end of one of the military trucks blossomed with smoke.

CHAPTER 14

"Hurry! Hurry! Hurry!" Nate urged Ashley. "As soon as they figure out it's only a smoke bomb, they'll start wondering why. And we need to be gone by then."

Ashley ran toward the back door of the trailer, carrying what she could.

Nate helped her up.

He ran back for the robots. One by one he lifted them into the trailer. He threw her his duffel bag. That left only me in the wheelchair.

Nate rolled me forward. With a loud grunt he picked both me and the wheelchair up and hoisted me into the trailer. Then he hopped up and swung both doors, putting us into temporary darkness.

"I think we're safe." His voice echoed in the trailer.

A lurch told us the truck was moving forward.

I held my breath.

If any of the soldiers were going to stop the truck, it would be in the next minute as it left this parking area.

I heard rumbling as the truck gained speed.

And finally, when I could hold my breath no longer, I relaxed.

We were on the highway.

Light hit us from the front of the trailer as a door opened.

It revealed stacks of heavy crates between the front and us. The outline of a man showed in the light. The man walked toward us on a small catwalk that led from the cab to the trailer. Nate had told us earlier that these newer trucks included sleeping quarters in the trailer.

"Not even close, Nate," came his deep voice. "No hitches. Just like the old days. Nothing like a good old smoke bomb to distract the enemy, huh?"

"Whistler was one of the best bomb guys I had," Nate said quietly. "We called him Whistler because he whistled all the time but couldn't carry a tune in a bucket. Still, I'd trust him with my life."

Whistler reached us. Nate shook his hand. In the dimness I could barely see his face, but I could tell he was African-American.

"Ashley and Tyce," Nate said proudly, "this is Whistler."

Whistler's white teeth showed in a wide grin as he shook both our hands. "Ee-yew. You guys don't smell that pretty, let me tell you. How long you been in the swamps?"

"Too long," Nate said with a laugh.

"Is there another driver?" I asked.

"No," Whistler answered. "Should there be?"

"You're back here and . . ." I'd never been in a truck before, but even I knew that someone should be at the steering wheel.

"Mag-strips," Whistler said.

"Mag-strips?"

"You from another planet, kid?" Whistler joked.

Here we go again, I thought, disgusted.

"Everyone knows how mag-strips work," Whistler continued.

"Go easy on him, Whistler," Nate said quickly. "He asks crazy questions, but I know he's not stupid." Then he turned to me. "All the interstate highways have mag-strips embedded every five feet in the pavement. They read computer sensors in the truck's axles. Between GPS and the main computer at the trucking company's head office, the trucks are guided at the right speed the right distance apart."

"This truck can be tracked anywhere it goes?"

"Tracked and guided. But only on the interstate highways. The drivers are needed everywhere else."

"Yeah," Whistler announced, "it's a great job for long-haul drivers. Once we get our rigs from the city streets or the truck stops onto the highway, we can kick back and relax."

He jerked his thumb toward the rear of our trailer. "Except for the Combat Force drivers we left back at the truck stop. They're under such tight computer supervision, they can't even blink without some commander knowing it. Which is a waste, considering they always travel in a pack of 10 trucks. What's one of the drivers going to do? Peel off and try to drive away from the escort trucks? Not even a payload of tantulem is worth that kind of risk."

"Tantulem?" I echoed.

"This kid *is* from Mars, isn't he?" Whistler joked to Nate. "Tantulem. The miracle metal they've been mining from the moon. Those trucks you saw back there? All of them came from the Everglades space base. That's where the shuttles land with tantulem from the Earth-Moon orbits."

Whistler paused. "Where exactly are you guys from? All Nate told me was he needed to get you out of this area."

"More important than where they are from," Nate interrupted, "is for me to know where they are going. Which is something they refused to tell me until we made it out of the Everglades. Now would be as good a time as any, Tyce."

"Not so fast," I said. "When can we get to the nearest library?"

CHAPTER 15

After about four hours on the interstate, we stopped at a motel just off the road.

Whistler rented a room near the back of the motel and parked his truck in such a way that passersby wouldn't see inside the trailer as he opened the back doors. During our time on the highway, Nate had given us a couple of reasons why we should stop, and Ashley and I saw no reason to disagree.

Especially for reason number one.

Showers! After a couple of days in prison and our time in the Everglades, we needed it.

Nate carried me into the room. Ashley followed. She went into the bathroom first while Nate and I waited in the outer room and watched television. Then my turn.

I loved it. Whistler had made sure to rent a room that would accommodate my needs from a wheelchair. It was the first shower I'd ever been able to take without worrying how much water I was using. On Mars, water was far too scarce, so we were only allowed showers twice a month. The rest of the time we used an evaporating gel as soap.

Here, under the hot water that streamed down like it

would never end, I couldn't believe that people on Earth had a luxury like this any day they wanted. I finally finished when I heard banging on the bathroom door.

Then Nate's turn.

He went in with his duffel bag while Ashley and I flipped channels. We'd never actually used a television before— she because of her time in the Institute, and me because of my time on Mars. I was familiar with a lot of the programs, though, from the DVD-gigaroms I'd watched on Mars.

The television hung from the ceiling, so Ashley and I could each lie on a bed and watch.

After I flipped through all the channels twice, Nate stepped out of the bathroom. But he didn't look like Nate.

"Wow!" Ashley said.

"Is that you?" I asked.

Nate had given himself a haircut and shaved his beard. Plus, he'd changed from his crusty wilderness clothing into a black turtleneck and tan pants. I almost didn't recognize him.

"Yes, it's me," Nate said. "We're on the run. Last thing I want is to draw attention to ourselves by looking like a hermit."

I kept flipping channels as he spoke.

"Whistler's not back yet?" he asked.

The truck was still outside, but Nate had asked Whistler to take a taxi to a car rental place to rent a van in Nate's name.

"He—" Ashley stopped as a car horn beeped outside. She smiled. "He's right here."

"Good," Nate said. "I'll say good-bye to him for all of us. You guys wait here while I unload the stuff from the trailer to the van. Then the three of us can travel by ourselves."

"Hang on!" I shouted. It felt like my eyes were bugging out of my head as I pointed at the television.

"Yes?" Nate looked confused. Filling the screen was the face of an old man handling a press conference.

"It's him!"

"Sure it's him. It's big news, this week's annual gathering of the Governors of Justice. In New York."

"You have television in your cabin in the Everglades?" Ashley asked.

"No. Radio."

"Oh," she said.

"You don't get it," I told them. This wasn't the time for idle conversation. "It's him!"

"What's the big deal?" Nate put in. "Everybody knows who he is. The Supreme Governor. Head of the Governors of Justice. Aside from the President of the World United Federation, he's the most powerful man in the world."

"But it's him!" I claimed excitedly. "The guy my dad held hostage in the Combat Force prison!"

CHAPTER 16

A half hour later we were on the interstate again, where GPS and an onboard computer system in the van guided us among the other vehicles through the mag-strip sensors embedded in the pavement.

I looked around. All I saw were large trucks, cars, and vans traveling at precisely the same speed we were, since the computer system maintained the proper distance between each vehicle.

Trees and hanging vines formed walls of green on both sides of the interstate. Over the previous hours of travel, the highway had lost some of its flatness and straightness. Nate had promised that as we traveled farther north, the surroundings would change even more.

"Do you like your library?" Nate asked, turning from behind the steering wheel to Ashley and me in the back of the van.

"Library?" I asked.

"Sure."

I was so used to Nate with a beard, it was strange to see his smile surrounded by smooth skin. "I know you're carrying a comp-board. We'll just plug it in to the Internet as we drive. You can find anything you need."

I sure hoped he was right.

"You know we have a comp-board?" Ashley repeated.

"Of course. Think I'd take you guys anywhere without searching all of your possessions while you slept? I was disappointed I needed a password to access the information."

It made me glad I hadn't gone into my diary earlier.

"That's not fair," Ashley said.

"Who said I had to be fair? We've got two different branches of military after us. My ex-commander and your prison people. But you won't tell me why. You want me to take you somewhere, but you won't give me the location. You won't even tell me why you were held in prison, or what those robots are for. Plus, I've been offered a lot of money for you. By Cannon. And by you guys. Which leads me to another thing. How you have that much money. Face it, there's a lot of questions about all of this. I'd be dumb not to find out what I can."

"I still don't think it's fair." Ashley frowned.

Nate gave her a charming grin. "As long as you don't kick me in the shins again."

"Guys?" I interrupted. "Library?"

"One wireless Internet connection is up front here," Nate said, still grinning as Ashley kept giving him a dirty look. "And there's another in the back beside your wheel-chair."

"We'll take the one in the back where you can't watch," I said, returning the same kind of grin he gave us. "We'd hate for you to find out anything else until we were ready."

"All right," I whispered to Ashley. The hum of the pavement beneath the van's wheels would screen our conversation from Nate. "I know we spent hours and hours talking about this on the spaceship, but I want to be sure I've got it right. All you saw was 'Arker,' right?"

"It was night," she said, sitting directly beside my wheelchair. "Remember, they had me drugged with something when they took me out of there. I could barely keep even one eye open. It was like a real bad fever, where you're not sure if what you are seeing is real or not. We got on a highway, and there was this skinny green sign. I think it said Arker 11."

"Eleven miles to a town or city called Arker." That's what Dad had guessed during our discussions on the *Moon Racer*. "And you said red mountains, almost like Mars."

"Yes." Her voice was quiet as she remembered.

In a way, her childhood had not been much different from mine. She'd been raised in the Institute, trapped in a canyon, never seeing anything of the rest of the world. I, of course, had seen just as little of the Earth.

We had done a map search on board, using the *Moon Racer*'s computer and one of the library's encyclopedia DVD-gigaroms. Dad had guessed red mountains to be somewhere in the southwestern states. But there was no Arker in Arizona, California, Colorado, Nevada, New Mexico, or Utah.

We weren't, however, without hope. Dad had wanted to do an Internet search as soon as we reached Earth. Of casinos.

"Slipper, Slipper, here we come," I said to Ashley.

"It could have been my imagination," she warned. "I

mean, I was drugged and fading quickly. And there it was, a giant red slipper in the sky. To me, it was named Casi. The last thing I saw before I woke up on a space shuttle, headed for Mars."

Unlike Dad, Ashley and I would never have guessed that *Casi* might be the first four letters of the word *Casino.* Or that the giant red slipper in the sky might be a neon sign. Not with our limited experience of Earth things.

I entered the words *slipper* and *casino* into the search directory. Seconds later my screen began to fill with results.

"Here it is," I said, scanning my computer screen. "Lucky Slipper. Red Slipper. Another Lucky Slipper. Another. And another."

I sighed as the search results finished.

"Ashley, there must be 100 results here. Casinos in Arizona, California, Colorado, Nevada, New Jersey, Montana." My Earth geography was limited to what I had memorized as part of my school lessons, but even I knew that all the states I was seeing were hundreds and thousands of miles apart. We only had four more days after today. How could we reach them all on the vague hope that Ashley would recognize something familiar?

"Hey," she exclaimed. "Look!"

I looked above her pointing finger. Near the top of the list. *Red Slipper Casino, Parker, Arizona.*

"Parker?" I whispered. "Not Arker?"

"They've got a link to their own Web site. Take a look."

I clicked. Waiting for the visual seemed to take forever.

Slowly a photo of a giant red slipper glowing in the night filled the screen.

"Ashley?"

"Scary." She shivered. "It's bringing all the bad memories of that night back to me again."

"Ashley!" It was my turn to point. Brochure information lined the bottom of the screen.

Located on the Colorado River, the Red Slipper Casino is a favorite stopping place for vacationers who visit nearby Lake Havasu. The reddish mountains nearby serve as a beautiful backdrop to a place of warm hospitality. . . .

"Reddish mountains!" she said, evidently seeing what I saw.

"Nate!" I shouted. "How far is it to Arizona from here?"

"Three days by highway," he answered. "But I have to tell you, I never intended on taking this van much farther than it will go on a tank of gas."

Without his help, we had no chance. How else could we transport two robots and someone in a wheelchair? Especially across the country? Especially with so few days left?

"Is it because we haven't given you any money yet?" I asked, ready to beg. "If you need to go to a bank—"

"Relax," he called back to me. "I have no intention of seeing either of you use your money cards."

Fear sickened my stomach.

Wild Man continued to speak to us from the front. "Don't you think they would use the computer record of where you spent or withdrew money to track your progress and find you?"

He didn't give us the chance to answer his question. "So I'm going to have to dip into my own accounts until all of this settles."

"Won't they be able to track you by your money trail?" I asked.

"Not a chance," Nate said firmly. "When I went into hiding, I set up fingerprint identities on three secret accounts.

They might have been able to find me in the swamps, but not my money. That's a good thing. Because let me tell you, the next part of our trip might cost a big chunk of money."

CHAPTER 17

"How does $50,000 sound?" Nate asked the woman standing beside him. Ashley and I remained in the van, peeking and listening through an open window.

"Sounds like too much," came a gravelly voice. The woman looked a little younger than my mom, and her name was Red. I easily understood why. Her deep red hair glinted like fire in the afternoon sun. Freckles covered all of her exposed skin, including neck, face, and strong-looking forearms that stuck out from her rolled-up blue sleeves.

"I want you to get $50 because we're old friends," Nate bargained. "You're telling me you want less?"

"No, I'm telling you I would want more."

"Let me get this straight. I offer $50. You say it sounds like too much. But you want more."

Behind us came the roar of an airplane engine. I twisted my head to peer out the other window of the van. Heat waves shimmered off a long, black runway cut into the trees. A small, single-jet airplane approached, twisting slightly as it angled to land, the air whooshing through the turbines in the plane's nose.

We had made it into the northern half of Florida, to this

small private airport. Nearby hangars held parked airplanes. Other than the runway and the hangars, the airport had a small trailer used as an office. That's where we had parked. Nate had gone in to talk to Red, and they'd stepped out here into the sunshine a few minutes later.

"Sure, I would want more," Red answered Nate's question. "That's if I even rented it to you. You've got two kids in a rented van, and once you get in the air I have no way of knowing where you are headed or when you'll be back. And you offer me triple what I would expect for a couple days' use of an airplane. That makes me worried."

"So worried that you won't trust a man who spent seven years with you in the same platoon?" Nate asked quietly.

"I owe you my life," Red said. "I haven't forgotten that. Which is why I'm not going to make a call back to the Combat Force goons who stopped by here yesterday asking about you."

"What!"

"I don't believe what they're saying about you. And I don't want to know the details either. But that's the other reason I'm worried. You're on the run. My guess is that the Combat Force is checking all your old friends, because we're the ones you would turn to. And if you're on the run, I can't rent you one of the airport's planes. Even for more than $50,000."

"You know I can fly anything," Nate argued. "And you'll get the airplane back. If anything happens to it, I'll cover the cost of the damage. You have my word on it."

"Your word is as good as gold," Red agreed. "Everyone in the platoon knew that. But I still can't rent you an airplane. If the Combat Force comes back and does a check on my records, they'll know two things. That I didn't call back when you showed up. And that I helped you escape.

After the way they threatened me yesterday . . . I mean, with my husband dead, I can't do much for my kids if I spend time in jail."

"Yeah." Nate sighed. "I heard about your husband and the car accident. I was real sorry for you. I understand. I can't put you in that kind of position. I appreciate you sticking your neck out to tell me they're on the lookout for us."

Red shrugged. "Not a big deal. You remember Skids? The skinny guy in the platoon who was lousy with directions?"

"Yeah."

"He runs a car dealership on the other side of the state. Who would have guessed, huh? Makes millions, and I remember he needed help tying his laces."

Nate laughed. "Who would have guessed?"

"Anyway," Red continued, "he called me yesterday. Said the Combat Force had dropped in on him too."

"Not good."

"Here's what's really strange," Red added. "Remember Cannon?"

"No one forgets a platoon commander, Red. He's a general now. One of the highest-ranking generals in the Combat Force."

"Yeah," Red returned. "Get this. Cannon showed up *after* the other Combat Force soldiers came around with questions. Alone. It was like he wasn't working with his own people. Skids told me the same thing, that Cannon showed up after the others. Now does that make sense to you?"

"Not much makes sense to me anymore," Nate answered.

"Tell you what," Red continued. "I'm going to give Skids a call. He owes you a favor too. I'll ask him to tell the Combat Force you stopped by there trying to buy a car from him cheap. They'll swarm that side of the state looking for you. You'll have a lot easier time escaping in the other direction. It's the least we can do for you."

How much good will that really do us to escape the Combat Force but still be in the van? I wondered. As Nate had told us earlier, the only chance of getting to Arizona on time was by airplane. But this was the only place Nate had a chance of getting one. And now it looked like that chance was cut off. We needed the airplane or else . . .

I thought of Dad waiting and waiting in the prison cell. I thought of the countdown of passing days. I felt a sharp pain in my palms and saw that I was clenching my fists so hard in frustration that my nails cut into my skin.

"See ya, Red," Nate told her.

"See ya, Nate."

Nate began to open the driver's-side door of the van, but Red's next words stopped him.

"Be a shame, wouldn't it," Red told Nate, her back to him, "if someone knew that the hangar at the end of the runway had a twin Otter with the door unlocked and the keys in it. It's an old beater hanging around, a relic from the old days, but it still runs really well."

Red turned toward Nate and grinned. "Be even more of a shame if someone knew that twin Otter airplane was fueled and ready to go, like it had been parked there for someone to take on short notice ever since those Combat Force goons showed up and threatened me not to help you. Biggest shame of all is that I might not even notice the twin Otter was gone for a few days, and by the time I filed the paperwork on it, who knows, that someone might even have returned it."

"Real shame," Nate agreed. He smiled.

Red reached out and shook Nate's hand. "Thanks for trusting me enough to come here. I still owe you plenty."

I wasn't sure if I understood what I'd just heard.

"Got to be going," Red finished. "My favorite show just started. Inside the trailer, I really have to crank the volume on my television to hear it above my air-conditioning unit. Shoot—when I'm in there watching, it's so loud, planes can come and go and I don't have any idea of what's happening out on the runway."

Nate got into the van. He started the engine.

"By the way," Red told him through the open window, "there's a little trail behind that hangar that leads into the trees. I suspect if anyone ever drove a couple hundred yards down that trail with a rented van, it would be weeks before anyone noticed where it was parked."

"Thanks," Nate said.

"Thanks for what?" Red grinned again. "I have no idea what you're talking about. Right? Not a thing."

CHAPTER 18

What an incredible world!

We flew in the twin Otter at 2,500 feet, low enough to see the changing terrain. As the hours passed in the airplane and as I traced our westward path on a map, Nate pointed out different landmarks. The three of us were equipped with headsets that let us speak and hear easily above the roar of the twin prop engines.

Less than 20 minutes after takeoff, we'd reached the Gulf of Mexico. With the beauty of the clouds and sun and the endless stretch of light bouncing off the whitecaps of the waves below, I'd hardly been able to breathe.

Then we'd cut back over land, crossing Alabama. Everywhere I looked, it was green. I was staggered to think of all the life that swarmed the earth and the sky and the water. Later, after refueling, we had crossed the Mississippi. I'd been unable to comprehend a flow of water hundreds upon hundreds upon hundreds of miles long, all of it filled with fish and insects and frogs and turtles.

Then the landscape had slowly changed, as the carpet of green trees began to break into open areas and we began to cross the Great Plains. Nate told us that less than 200 years earlier, millions of buffalo had lived there, and I tried to imagine the immense herds in a sea of waving grass.

We had to stop after the first day of flying, because Nate didn't want to fly at night in the mountains. I didn't understand why he wanted to be cautious until we began to fly again the next morning.

At first, the mountains were just blue smudges across the horizon ahead of us. Then the snowcapped peaks came into focus. And then we were in them, with Nate following highways below us so that we could make it through the passes. Wind shook us from side to side until our wingtips seemed to brush the snow and the granite. It was strange to imagine our plane as just a little speck floating high above the pine forests and rivers.

Time and again on our journey I stared—and wondered what it would have been like to grow up on Earth and to be able to see this incredible world every single day.

As we reached the other side of the mountains, moving into the western half of New Mexico and finally into Arizona, the red rocks and brown valleys reminded me in a small way of Mars.

When I thought of Mars, I thought about Mom. I wondered if she knew somehow that Dad was in trouble.

And I thought about Dad.

Especially of the fact that, including today, there were only four days left of our countdown.

And I began to pray. I asked God to give us courage for whatever else we needed to do to save Dad and rescue the other kids, who were as trapped as Ashley had been.

"There's the Parker Dam!" Nate pointed out the window to our left. "And downriver, the town of Parker."

He banked the airplane as I checked the map. To our right, a long, narrow lake bounced brilliant blue light from the reds and browns of the desert. This was Lake Havasu, formed by the Parker Dam. On the other side of the dam, the Colorado River was a snake of blue winding through more desert reds and browns. From the air, the town of Parker appeared to be a neatly laid grid of miniature houses.

"Anything look familiar yet?" Nate asked Ashley.

When we had stopped last night, Ashley and I had agreed that we at least had to trust Nate enough to fill him in on a few details. Then he might be able to help us pinpoint our search. And so we had.

Now Ashley shook her head. Ashley hadn't spoken much over the last few hours. I wondered if she was afraid to return to the place where she had spent most of her life. Now it would seem like a prison to her. But then—among the others who, like her, had been in the Institute as long as they could remember—she didn't know any other kind of life. Then her life had seemed normal.

"I'll take us in a few circles," Nate said. "I know things look different in the air than from the ground, but you never know."

All Ashley had been able to tell us last night was that the children could see a strange tall mountain peak from the open area where they were allowed to play. She said all the kids had called it the "Unsleeping Soldier" because it looked like it guarded them.

Twenty minutes later we were still circling. The red mountains threw dark shadows into deep canyons.

"I'm going to have to take us down," Nate announced into our headsets. "We'll find a place to stay for the night. Tomorrow we'll drive around in a rented vehicle and keep looking."

Tomorrow. One more day closer to the deadline.

"Hang on!" Ashley shouted. "There!"

Sure enough, one of the peaks did look like a tall, skinny man.

"There?" Nate repeated.

"There!" Ashley insisted.

"Check it out, Tyce." Nate motioned toward the map.

I studied the map briefly, then circled a place with my pencil. "Makes sense. Abandoned military base," I said, reading the map. "No trespassing."

"Exactly. I think we've found it," Nate said enthusiastically. "First thing tomorrow, we'll check it out."

Which would have been a great plan.

Except as we were watching television in our motel room late that evening, there was a sharp crack of breaking glass.

I caught a glimpse of a small ball as it tumbled across the floor.

Nate dove for it, but it was too late.

The flash of light and the boom of the explosion came at the same time.

And when the bitter smoke hit my face, I gagged once, then sank into blackness.

CHAPTER 19

I woke up in my wheelchair with a dry mouth and a slight headache.

A breeze came in through the broken window. It was still dark outside, and the clock in the motel room read 3:15 A.M. The television was still on, with the volume turned down. Its dim glow showed that Nate had been duct-taped to one chair. He was blinking himself awake too. Ashley lay on the floor, where she had fallen out of her chair in front of the television. She was still unconscious.

A large man in army fatigues stood against the door. Shaved bald, he had a square face with a bent nose. The neuron gun in his right hand was pointed at Nate.

"You're getting soft and old," the man behind the neuron gun snorted to Nate. "I really expected you to be somewhere in the desert, in a camp guarded by trip lines. This is the price you pay for wanting a place with beds and showers. The Wild Man I remembered from the platoon never would have made the mistake of bunking down where he could be so easily trapped."

The man continued to speak as he shrugged. "But then,

the Wild Man I knew never would have turned traitor. Who paid you and how much?"

"Why would I need to be paid to keep you from getting your hands on these kids?" Nate answered in a level voice. "It's obvious now that *you're* the one who means them harm."

"Me?"

"Give me a break, Cannon. These kids have robots. And they're on the run from a Combat Force base and prison. That alone tells me they have something so valuable that they need help. And somehow I don't think you represent official channels here. Otherwise there would be Combat Force soldiers with you and we'd already be outside and loaded into a military truck. You wouldn't have come to me in the Everglades with your little plan to steal them as they escaped from that prison either."

"Ashley, Tyce, pardon my manners for beginning a conversation without letting you know who this is," Nate said, spreading his arms wide, making a mockery of his elaborate introduction of the man with the neuron gun. "General Jeb McNamee. Known as Cannon, because when we were friends—*when* we were friends—I liked to call him a big shot. But I guess our friendship is now over, because I refuse to like anyone who would mean you two any harm."

So this was Cannon, the general who had first approached Nate and given him the equipment and timetable to capture us from the swamp boat.

"*Me* mean them harm? I'm trying to *rescue* them from the Combat Force," the general snapped. "Something that would have been a lot easier if you hadn't run with them. So let me ask you again. Who paid you? The Terratakers? Because if I find out you had anything to do with my son being taken away from me—"

"General, somewhere you've been out in the sun too long without a hat."

Without warning, the general pulled the trigger of his neuron gun.

I saw and heard nothing. Neuron guns don't make noise. But Nate tilted in his chair and groaned slightly as he fell back into unconsciousness. The neuron blast would have paralyzed half his muscles. I doubted he'd wake for another 20 minutes.

"You OK?" the general asked me.

"Yes, but—"

"Hang on." He stepped past me and returned from the motel bathroom with a glass of water. In my thirst I reached for it, but he was already past me again. He knelt beside Ashley, who was struggling to sit up. He put his arm behind her back and helped her stand. "Sorry about the punch of that sleeping gas, but I couldn't see any other way to neutralize Nate without putting you both in danger."

Ashley gulped back the water.

"I trust you are here because it's close to the Institute?" the general asked. "I mean, when Nate stopped to refuel the airplane yesterday, he didn't go to the trouble of buying a van like he did here."

Like I was going to answer this man?

"I wouldn't mind some water myself," I said from the wheelchair. I had a plan. Not much of one. But the best I could think of.

The general walked into the bathroom again. I rolled forward to block the doorway and turned my head back to Ashley.

"Run!" I whispered to Ashley. "Get the motel manager to call for help!"

Ashley was groggy as she got to her feet. She took a

step to the door as the general came out of the bathroom with a full glass of water.

"Hey!" he said from behind my wheelchair as she reached the door.

He dropped the water and tried pushing my wheelchair out of his way. I grabbed his belt.

"Go!" I shouted at Ashley. "Go!"

She struggled to unbolt the door.

The general swept my hand and wheelchair aside and dived forward. He yanked her away from the door.

"Are you guys crazy?" he said, gently pushing her back toward the center of the room. "Why are you trying to escape when I finally managed to rescue you?"

"Rescue us? You sent Nate to kidnap us," I pointed out. "He's helping us run away from you."

"What!"

"I doubt you have good intentions. There's no way you should have known when and where we were leaving the prison," I continued. "You must be working with Dr. Jordan."

"Now you're telling me you don't even trust your own father." When this man with the huge ugly face frowned, it was not a sight that would help little children sleep better.

"Of course we trust him." Ashley put her hands on her hips in her trademark pose. It was clear she wasn't scared by the general in his army fatigues.

"Then why run with Nate?" the general said. "You know that your father and the Supreme Governor set this up."

Silence.

The general studied my face. Then Ashley's.

"I said," the general repeated, "you know that your father and the Supreme Governor set this up. Including the tracking device in your arm. And the money cards that would let us watch your progress if anything went wrong. It was in your father's letter. It had instructions telling you that it was safe for Nate to deliver both of you to me. And I was to help you keep out of the hands of the Combat Force as we found the Institute."

The letter.

"Nice try," I said sarcastically. My dad's cell *had* been wired. The Combat Force knew Dad had given me a letter. This man could easily be making this up.

"Nice try?" he repeated. "Now I need to convince you that your father . . ." The general shook his head. "Kid, how else would I have known when you would be released? The Supreme Governor set all of this up. Including insisting on visiting your father personally in his cell. That way he could quickly explain to your father what he needed to do, through a handwritten note that couldn't be picked up on the audio, and then get your father's help. The Supreme Governor allowed himself to be taken as your dad's hostage, securing your release from the base."

Is that why Dad had the dull edge of the blade pressed against the old man's throat?

"And while you were in your dad's cell, the Supreme Governor jabbed a tracking chip into your arm. That allowed me to pick up from there, once you were away from the base and in the boat."

I remembered the old man grabbing my arm and the stabbing pain. I remembered wondering why Dad had pretended to be angry. All of that to plant a tracking chip?

My face must have been an open book of confusion.

"Tracking chip. That's how I found you," the general explained. "I've been following you guys for two days, just waiting for the right time to move in. Come on. All of it was in the letter. You did read your dad's letter. Right?"

Only two people knew I hadn't read that letter. Me. And Ashley, whom I had just told a few hours ago, while Nate was taking a shower and Ashley and I were watching television.

Besides Ashley, only one person knew the letter had been destroyed by water. Me.

Which meant the general had no reason to bluff me. He really thought I *had* read the letter. He really thought I knew all the stuff he was telling us.

My words came out as if my tongue were a block of wood. "You mean that you *were* sent by my dad? And that Nate was sent by you?"

"Stop playing games," the general snapped. "I had to send Nate because there are too many Terratakers in the Combat Force. If any of them found out I was behind this mission to rescue you, it was too possible for this information to reach the Terratakers. And with them holding my son hostage, there was too much danger he would die."

He pointed at Nate, disgust on his face. "It was a good plan, until Nate turned traitor and took off with you both. That cost us a lot of time. And now we're down to a few days before all of it happens."

"All of what?"

Now it was the general's turn to be confused. "That's part of it. We don't know quite what, just that Jordan has planned something big. And bad. You know that, too, otherwise—"

My face must have looked blank.

"You did read the letter, didn't you?"

"It, um . . . fell into . . . the swamp when we were being chased." I stopped. "No, I didn't read it."

Comprehension smoothed out the concerned wrinkles on the general's face. "No wonder Nate believed he was rescuing you from me. No wonder you have no idea what is waiting for us."

"Waiting for us?" I said. I gave him a weak smile. "Is there any chance you can prove my father sent you?"

He nodded. "It's about time you asked. Does the phrase 'Twinkie nose' ring a bell?"

I winced. "Yes."

"Twinkie nose?" Ashley asked. "Isn't a Twinkie a—"

"Yes, yes," I said quickly. "But that's all I'm telling."

When I was too little to remember, my mom said she'd catch me picking my nose so often it was like I was trying to eat a Twinkie, which she'd explained was an Earth snack. When I was old enough to be embarrassed about this, if I misbehaved in public, she would threaten to call me Twinkie Nose and explain why to everybody listening. That always settled me down.

"So now you know your father sent me, right?" the general said.

I nodded. "Do you think you could start from the beginning? With all the stuff in the letter that I didn't get a chance to read?"

CHAPTER 20

A couple of hours later, dawn broke across the hills. The sky was rose colored, with a hint of orange growing brighter as the sun almost broke across the jagged lines of the horizon.

We drove on the main highway in a van that Nate had purchased from a used-car dealer. The small town of Parker and the motel were only a few minutes behind us, but already the desert was totally without any houses or signs or any other marks of human life. There was no other traffic. Because the sand was almost red, it felt like we were on Mars. The weight of gravity, however, and my tiredness told me otherwise.

"Let me get this straight," Nate, now partially recovered from the neuron blast, said. He sat up front, in the passenger seat. "The Supreme Governor set this up."

Nate had only been awake for a few minutes. We'd left the motel quickly, taking time only to load up the van with all our gear and the robots and pay the bill.

"From the beginning," Cannon said, not taking his eyes off the road as he drove. "We even planned it down to the tracking chip in Tyce's arm. Without that, I'd have never found you."

"Why is the Supreme Governor involved?" Nate asked, incredulous. "I mean, he's the most powerful government person in the world. What does he—"

"His grandson is in the Institute. Just like my son," the general replied harshly.

Grandson? Son? I had a dozen questions of my own. But I kept my mouth shut and listened.

"We shouldn't have been arrested when we arrived on Earth," Ashley said. "It was Dr. Jordan who tried to kill us. *He's* the one who should have been put in prison."

"Some of us know that now," Cannon answered. He didn't turn his head as he drove. His neck seemed like chiseled granite.

"Who is 'us'?" Nate interrupted.

"A group of the top World United Federation Combat Force generals. You see, as the *Moon Racer* approached Earth, the signals sent to the Combat Force informed us that the ship's pilot and some of the crew had turned against two high-level government passengers, including Dr. Jordan. They'd been killed and ejected into space."

That was exactly what Dad had informed me in his note.

"A total lie," I said indignantly. "It was the opposite. Dr. Jordan and Luke Daab had complete control of the ship's computer. They must have secretly changed all of our regular transmissions."

"We know that now, but how could we tell differently at the time? Furthermore, we had no way of knowing that Dr. Jordan was alive and on his way to Earth. Since then, we've confirmed that. Intelligence sources tell us a cargo ship returning from the Moon picked up his escape pod. From there, Dr. Jordan has disappeared."

*And now he's somewhere on Earth, planning something
we have to stop. Only we don't quite know what.*

"What changed?" Nate asked quietly. I could tell his old
belief in his platoon commander was back. "How did you
find out the truth and decide that the report was false?"

"Two things. The first was Tyce's computer."

My computer?

"Naturally we went through all the confiscated equipment. Including Tyce's computer. A program broke his
password code. It had a diary of the *Moon Racer*'s journey.
That gave us a different story of the space trip. We weren't
sure whether to believe it, but it cast enough doubt that
when prisoner Blaine Steven asked for a private meeting
with the Supreme Governor, we arranged it."

"Blaine Steven . . ." Nate prompted.

"Former director of the Mars Project. A man with plenty
of political clout even though he hadn't been on Earth for
over a decade."

Blaine Steven. The man who'd secretly been working for
Dr. Jordan all those years he'd been on Mars. And yet, once
aboard the *Moon Racer,* Steven had been worried that Dr.
Jordan would try to kill him. For good reason.

"Blaine Steven," Cannon continued, "didn't know the
details, only that Dr. Jordan intended some kind of
Terrataker mission as soon as he got back to Earth. And
with all of the rest of what Blaine Steven told us, things
began to make sense. We are now trying our best to stop
Jordan, but we're working in the dark. That's why we need
Tyce and Ashley so badly. It goes way beyond trying to rescue my own son and the governor's grandson."

Cannon began to slow down.

In the growing light of day, I could hardly recognize the
upcoming turnoff as a road. It was more like a set of tire

tracks leading into the desert hills. Cannon drove off the highway onto the tracks.

"Cannon," Nate said quietly, "where we need to go, this van doesn't have a chance."

"We're not going there in the van. Remember, I do have a few military connections."

"Which is why the Supreme Governor brought you into this?" Nate asked.

The van bounced and jolted. Dust began to film the windows.

"He brought me into this because he could trust me. As you well know, like most high levels of the Federation government, even the top levels of our Combat Force are infiltrated by Terrataker rebels. Just like Dr. Jordan. With crucial peace talks coming up in New York, the rebels are going out of their way to bring war. If any of the Terratakers found out about Tyce and Ashley and their robot connections, what we're about to do next would have no chance. That's why the Supreme Governor and I needed to arrange secretly to help Tyce and Ashley escape. And why I brought you in to help. I wanted you to bring them to me before the Combat Force could track them down again. We figured with Tyce and Ashley's help, we also might just find the secret location of the Institute."

"I think I'm with you," Nate said slowly. "These kids have refused to tell me anything about these robots, but I can make my guesses."

"As could the other generals who were about to arrive at the Combat Force prison. That was another reason for getting them out in a hurry."

"Sir?" I broke in. "What exactly *is* happening? All I know is that we're on a six-day countdown to find the Institute and then rescue my dad from the base. And today is day four."

Cannon glanced at his watch. "A very tight countdown. In a little over 48 hours, the Supreme Governor and the assembled governors of all the nations of the world will have their annual meeting in New York. It's a simple guess that if the Terratakers are going to try anything, this is the time. Especially if Dr. Jordan believes no one knows he is on Earth, and that no one knows about the Institute."

"Impossible to do any damage," Nate scoffed. "You of all people know how tightly secured the meeting will be. Nothing short of the world's best army would be able to get in there."

"Exactly," Cannon returned. "And that's exactly what Jordan has. From what Blaine Steven told us, his army can't be stopped."

The van rounded a corner into a tight canyon.

"Let me correct myself," Cannon added. "Jordan's army can't be stopped without Tyce and Ashley."

"How?" I asked. My knowledge of geography wasn't great, but even I knew that Arizona was a long way from New York.

"I wish I could stop right now and explain it all to you," Cannon answered. "But if you look ahead, you'll see our ride."

He pointed through the windshield. We saw a helicopter, painted dull green. Machine guns were mounted on each side.

"I've had the pilot on standby," Cannon said. "Right now every minute counts. You'll learn more when we get to the Institute. I just hope no one tries to shoot us down when we land."

CHAPTER 21

"There?" Cannon shouted a few minutes later.

"There!" Ashley said.

I focused a pair of binoculars where Cannon had pointed. Ahead and below was a box canyon, cut in a perfect square halfway up a mountain. It seemed empty.

I truly hoped it was.

I briefly set the binoculars down and glanced around me in the helicopter.

Nate squatted on one side, armed with a rocket launcher. Cannon guarded the other side with another rocket launcher. The pilot had his right hand on the trigger mechanisms of the helicopter's machine guns. He was a skinny guy with dark glasses who called himself Grunt. Military people sure liked weird nicknames.

I watched the three of them, tense and ready. If someone attacked as we landed, would we have enough firepower to defend the helicopter?

The helicopter moved in closer, chasing its own shadow across the barren rocks of the desert hills.

And slowly it began to take us down into the canyon of the Institute.

"Are you sure this is the right place?" Nate asked Ashley.

No one had stepped out of the helicopter yet. We were parked squarely in the middle of the empty canyon. Although the pilot had shut down the helicopter, the roar of the motor echoed in my ears, making the silence around us seem loud.

"I'm sure." Ashley pointed up at the high, narrow mountain peak. "I saw that every day I was allowed out here in the sunshine."

"What," Cannon said to Nate, "you're hoping someone shows up and starts shooting at us?"

"It just doesn't seem right," Nate commented. He had not taken his hands off the rocket launcher. "You'd think if there was something to guard, we wouldn't be able to just walk in like this."

"Fly," Cannon corrected. "It's not like this is easy to get to, even if you know where it is."

Cannon, of course, was right.

It had no entrance. This was not a natural canyon, but a perfect deep box cut into the rock. Only heavy machinery could have made this. It was too square, the sheer high walls too straight, and the ground too perfectly flat. On the far side, maybe 100 yards from the helicopter, was a large metal door set into the canyon wall.

Nate pointed at the door. "You've been in there, right, Ashley?"

"Every day I was here," she replied. "Inside it's like a maze of rooms. It's where we ate and slept and worked on computer simulations and robot control."

"We've got explosives," Cannon pressed. "We can blow the door apart."

"Then let's do it," Nate said. "We'll leave the kids behind."

I lifted the binoculars again while they began to unload their equipment. I studied the door. There seemed nothing strange about it.

Except for the dead lizard on the ground in front of it.

I looked closer, straining my eyes.

The lizard seemed to be lying on top of a dead bird.

Weird.

I put the binoculars down and said nothing because Nate and Cannon had already begun moving across the open floor of the box canyon. They each carried ready machine guns, with backpacks to carry the explosives.

I peered through the binoculars again.

A tiny mouse scurried up to the dead lizard. Was it going to eat it?

As I watched, the mouse stopped moving. It fell on its side.

Weird.

Nate's words came back to me. *You'd think if there was something to guard, we wouldn't be able to just walk in like this.*

"Hey!" I shouted at the two of them. "Hey!"

My loud, frantic words bounced off the high rock walls around us.

They stopped.

I waved them back.

"Yes?" Nate asked. Cannon's eyes didn't settle on me. He was too busy scanning in all directions for danger.

"Remember you thought it was strange that we could just walk in like this?"

Nate nodded.

"Well, what if it *is* guarded? But not by people."

"Trust me," Nate said, "we're keeping our eyes wide open."

"But you haven't been using the binoculars. Try them now. And look at the door from here."

Nate did as I requested. "Dead animals. Place like this, who knows how long they've been there?"

"The mouse just died," I said. "I saw it walk up to the lizard and keel over. I remember reading Earth stories about miners who brought a canary down with them. If it died . . ."

Nate locked eyes with me. ". . . maybe it was breathing poison gas. Gas leaking out from under the door."

"Exactly," I said. "Who knows what's on the other side of that door?"

"Great," he replied. "So how do we open it without killing ourselves?"

"You don't." I grinned. "Ashley and I do."

CHAPTER 22

"Ready?" Ashley asked.

"Ready," I said.

We sat in the helicopter, each of us plugged in to our bot-packs. Ashley was seat belted in place. Nate had strapped my arms onto my wheelchair. On short notice, it was the best we could do to remain motionless.

The bot-pack was a mobile computer unit. One end was attached to a plug that connected to my spinal nerves. The other end of the bot-pack fired X-ray waves to the computer controls on the robot.

The rules of robot control were simple. First, avoid any electrical currents—they could do serious damage to my own brain. Second, disengage instantly at the first warning of any damage to the robot's computer drive. Especially since my brain circuits worked so closely with the computer's circuits.

"Ready for the headset and blindfold," I told Nate.

He placed a soundproof headset on my ears and then a blindfold over my eyes. The fewer distractions to reach my brain in my real body, the better.

It was dark and silent while I waited for a sensation that

had become familiar and beautiful to me. The sensation of entering the robot computer.

My wait did not take long. Soon I began to fall off a high, invisible cliff into a deep, invisible hole.

I kept falling and falling and falling. . . .

The morning sun almost blinded me.

It didn't hit my own eyes, but one of the four video lenses of the robot parked outside the helicopters.

Beside it was the robot controlled by Ashley. We waved robot arms at each other to confirm we were both in control.

The lower body of each robot was much like my wheelchair. Instead of a pair of legs, an axle connected two wheels. Each robot's upper body was a short, thick hollow pole that stuck through the axle, with a heavy weight to counterbalance the arms and head. Within this weight was the battery that powered the robot.

Four video lenses served as eyes. Three tiny microphones took in sound; a speaker allowed our voices to be heard.

Since the computer drive of the robot was well protected within the hollow titanium pole, the robot could fall 10 feet without shaking the drive. The drive had a short antenna plug at the back of the pole to send and receive X-ray signals.

Ashley's robot rolled forward.

I followed across the hard-packed sand. For the first time since landing on Earth, I felt like I was in familiar territory. This was no different than traveling across the surface of Mars. To the robot, it didn't feel any different whether the atmosphere around it was oxygen or carbon dioxide.

Or poisonous gas.

Nate had slung a backpack over the right hand of my robot and given me a quick lesson on how to plant the explosive device.

If I made a mistake and blew it up too early at least it would take off the robot's hand instead of my own.

The door blew perfectly.

A green cloud of gas mushroomed outward and dispersed well before reaching the helicopter.

We'd been right about a booby trap.

Because Nate and Cannon worried about other traps, they had asked Ashley and me to first explore the inside of the Institute with our robots.

It was dark inside.

But that didn't matter.

Our robots were equipped with infrared. We didn't need light. And Ashley knew exactly where to go.

We didn't discover any more booby traps.

But we did find light switches.

And 23 kids.

They were in a room just down the hallway.

We halted in shock.

Large upright cylinders, made of clear plastic, were almost full of what looked like dark jelly. Wires and tubes ran down from the ceiling into each cylinder.

The 23 kids?

They couldn't talk to us. Couldn't wave at us. Couldn't see us. Or hear us.

Each was suspended in one of those cylinders of dark jelly. With only their heads above the jelly and with the tubes and wires running down into their bodies.

Although their eyes were closed, they weren't dead. Only unconscious.

The rest of the Institute was empty.

They'd been left behind.

Trapped in life-support systems.

CHAPTER 23

"Put me back!" the first kid pulled from a cylinder shouted. "Put me back!"

Another five minutes had passed since first opening the outer door.

Grunt, our pilot, was still with the helicopter. Nate and Cannon had gone ahead of Ashley and me, once we'd disconnected from our robots, and helped one of the kids out of a cylinder. They'd wrapped him in a blanket.

Ashley had followed me in my wheelchair to the room. We had arrived just as the kid woke up and started screaming.

"It's OK," Nate soothed, holding the kid. He was a little bigger than Ashley. His hair was dark and slick where some of that jelly stuff had touched him. "We're friends. We're here to help all of you."

"Put me back!" the kid screamed. His eyes rolled with panic. "If he knows I'm gone, he'll use the death chip! Put me back! Put me back!"

"Son!" Cannon said, leaning over to touch the boy's shoulder. "Son! We can't help you unless you tell us what is happening."

The kid's screams changed to pleading. "Please. Hook me up to my robot. He'll see it isn't responding. He'll think I'm refusing to help. And he'll trigger the death chip."

Ashley stepped forward. "Michael. It's me." She kneeled down beside him and took his hand.

"Ashley! You're back! They said you were dead!" Then Michael remembered his panic. "Ashley! Tell them to hook me up! You know how we work!"

"Michael, we need to know what's happening." Ashley spoke calmly.

"I don't have time to tell you! My robot is down right now. He'll—"

"Dr. Jordan?" Ashley asked.

"Yes! Yes! All of us. He implanted death chips. That's why we do what he tells us. Right now he might be talking to my robot and if it doesn't respond—" Michael began to sob with fear—"he'll activate the death chip and something in my heart will explode and . . ."

Nate spoke urgently to Ashley. "We really need to know what's happening here. If he can't tell us, I don't know what to do."

Ashley's eyes narrowed. "Michael, what if I hook up to your robot? Dr. Jordan will have no idea that you and I have switched. These men need to learn everything they can from you."

Michael shivered beneath his blanket. He said nothing for several long moments.

Finally he nodded.

"I got to ask you something first," Cannon said. His voice was down to a whisper. "I've looked at all the other kids, and I don't see him. Where's Chad?"

"Chad?" Michael repeated.

"My son," Cannon said. "And someone else. Brian. Both about your age."

"Don't know them," Michael said. Slowly. I guessed he could tell how worried the general was. "Chad? Brian?"

The general bowed his head. "They've got them somewhere else."

Nate put a big hand on the general's shoulder. "Remember, as hostages, they are more valuable alive."

The general took a deep breath before lifting his head. "You're right. And here's where we win the first battle in stopping them."

The general seemed to grow in strength. "Michael, tell us what you can."

"About four days ago," Michael began, "our keepers cleared out of here. One by one, each of us disappeared. Because one by one, they were taking us into this room and hooking us up."

Behind us Ashley was blindfolded and strapped motionless into a chair we'd found. One of the wires from the ceiling was the contact wire to a computer. It had a plug that fit into her spinal plug. The other tubes from the ceiling hung beside her, slowly dripping liquids.

"Hooking you up?" Nate said, as if he were trying to understand the robot-control system.

"Somewhere all 23 of these kids are controlling robots through virtual reality," I explained.

Michael nodded. "I can't tell you where the robots are, though. I just know that Dr. Jordan is there, supervising us while he waits. But he won't tell us what we're waiting for."

"If the robots aren't here and nearby," Cannon mumbled, more to himself than to Michael, "how can they possibly be controlled?"

"Satellite," I guessed. With my Mars background, I knew a lot about communication technology. "These high mountains are perfect for a transmitter to beam something to a satellite. Signals bouncing at the speed of light from the main computers here could reach anywhere in the world almost instantly."

Cannon's eyes bugged out. "You're telling me these 23 kids are capable of handling their robots anywhere in the world? From this hidden room here?"

"Yes, sir," I said. "I'm afraid that's true."

"It makes sense," Nate commented, stroking his now-stubbled chin. Then he pointed at the other cylinders with motionless kids on life support. "What scares me most is how permanent this looks."

"Permanent?" Cannon asked.

"I'm not a doctor," Nate answered Cannon, "but I do know that when people are in hospitals for long periods, they have to be shifted in their beds at least three times a day. Otherwise they develop horrible bedsores. This jelly stuff . . . it looks like that solves the problem. These kids have been set up in a way that no pressure will be put on their bodies. As long as those tubes supply them with nutrients, they will live in the cylinders indefinitely."

"You can't treat humans like this!" Cannon exploded. "What about sleep!"

"Michael?" Nate asked.

"We all fall asleep at the same time. We all wake up at the same time. And all of us have headaches when we wake. I've talked to some of the other kids—"

"How can you talk to them?" Cannon interrupted. "You're all here, suspended and unconscious on life support."

"Our robots talk to each other," Michael said quietly.

"Our bodies might not be moving here, but for 16 hours a day we live through the robot bodies, wherever those bodies are. Until we fall asleep again. And when we wake up, we see what the robot bodies let us see."

"Must give them some kind of sleeping drug," Nate reasoned. "Drip nutrients through the tubes. And when you want the kids to fall asleep, drip some kind of drug. Measure it right, and they'll wake up eight hours later. If a computer monitors all of this, you don't even need anybody around. Ever."

Cannon made a fist and punched his other palm. "So they've been left here. Like mushrooms. Too afraid to disobey because if they do, Jordan will activate a death chip that kills them in their bodies here."

Michael nodded. "It's worse than that."

"Worse?" Nate asked. "How could this be worse?"

"Here we mostly trained with digging robots. But when they put me in the jelly and I saw through robot eyes on the other side . . ."

"Yes," Cannon said with impatience.

"I was handling a soldier robot. And right now, Dr. Jordan is training us on how all of its weapons work. I'm not sure anything can stop these robots."

"Unbelievable," Cannon exclaimed. "These kids are the perfect military weapons. Hidden and untouchable. They control weapons that can be used anywhere in the world. They—"

Ashley suddenly spoke from her chair. "Tyce! Nate! Get me out of this blindfold. I need to talk."

Seconds later, Nate had unstrapped her. She yanked off her blindfold and blinked a few times. Shaking her hair, she ran her fingers through it.

"Nate," she called frantically, "can you unhook one of

the other kids and hook up Tyce? I'm going to need his help. I can't stay here any longer and tell you why. I've got to get back to my robot. Strap me in again."

Without waiting for permission, she pulled her blindfold down again. She slumped back in the chair as she resumed control of her robot.

"Tyce?" Nate asked.

I nodded.

Somewhere in the world was a small army of super-weapon robots. With Dr. Jordan in complete control. I would do everything I could to help Ashley stop him. I wasn't sure how we were going to do it, but I was determined to try. I knew now that Ashley was right. We were the kids' only chance. And now my dad's life hung in the balance too. Even more, what happened in the next 48 hours could change the world—for better or worse.

Five minutes later, I, too, was ready. I was strapped to my wheelchair, blindfolded, and put into a soundproof headset.

I didn't know what was on the other side.

But I was about to find out.

In the darkness and silence, I began to fall . . . fall . . . fall . . .

ARE YOU AN ALIEN?

Are you an alien? Bet no one ever asked you that before.

But in *Mission 7: Countdown,* that's exactly how Tyce feels. After all, he's spent his entire life on Mars—weird as it sounds—and has never seen Earth before. When he arrives on Earth, he's in awe. Just think of never having seen a yellow sun, white clouds, and a blue sky before, and then seeing them for the first time. Then add to that lots of other sights, like dogs, palm trees, tall grass, a variety of flowers. Sounds, like birds chirping, trucks on an interstate, and the roar of a male gator. Smells, like fish frying and the musty dampness of the Everglades. Surrounded by all these things you'd never experienced, your mouth would probably drop open too! You'd be overwhelmed. And who could blame you?

It wouldn't help, either, if somebody made fun of you, even in a teasing way, like Wild Man did to Tyce. "Where exactly are you from? Mars or something?" Little did Wild Man know how much his teasing bugged Tyce. How it hit home and made Tyce feel even more lonely and afraid. Because he *is* from another planet. And worse, he's the only true "Martian" on Earth. He's 50 million miles from his home—and everything he knows!

It's no wonder that all of a sudden the dome on Mars looks less scary. Even with all its regulations, like only getting a shower twice a month. Even with all its crises, such as the oxygen leak, a hostile takeover, and almost getting blown up by a black box. Why? Because Earth, as beautiful as it is, will never be Tyce's real home.

But in a real sense, you should stop and wonder whether Earth is *your* true home.

All of us have an emptiness that needs to be filled. Some people try to fill it with money or the pursuit of fun. This emptiness truly can make us feel like an alien; some people have described the emptiness as being "homesick for a place you've never been."

Where is that place? The place that lies beyond our life on Earth? Because of his growing faith in God, Tyce has discovered there's more to life than what meets the eye. Than what we can see and touch. He believes that neither Earth nor Mars is his final destination. Instead, someday he'll take an incredible flight to a place called heaven, where he'll live forever with God.

But that doesn't mean we take this beautiful Earth for granted. God wants us to enjoy it. So why not, for the next couple of days, pretend you're seeing everything on Earth for the first time? Like it's "one giant candy store," as Wild Man said. From plants to insects to reptiles and birds, explore how life swarms this world, cramming each nook and corner. Then you, too, might agree with Nate—that it takes more faith to deny the existence of God than to see a Creator behind all of this.

And then you'll also find it easier to see beyond this Earth to God's ultimate plan for us—to be with him in heaven someday.

ABOUT THE AUTHOR

Sigmund Brouwer, his wife, recording artist Cindy Morgan, and their daughter split living between Red Deer, Alberta, Canada, and Nashville, Tennessee. He has written several series of juvenile fiction and eight novels. Sigmund loves sports and plays golf and hockey. He also enjoys visiting schools to talk about books. He welcomes visitors to his Web site at www.coolreading.com, where he and a bunch of other authors like to hang out in cyberspace.

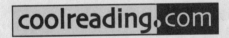

mars DIARIES

are you ready?

Set in an experimental community on Mars, the Mars Diaries feature 14-year-old Tyce Sanders. Life on the red planet is not always easy, but it is definitely exciting. As Tyce explores his strange surroundings, he also finds that the mysteries of the planet point to his greatest discovery—a new relationship with God.

MISSION 1: OXYGEN LEVEL ZERO
Can Tyce stop the oxygen leak in time?

MISSION 2: ALIEN PURSUIT
What attacked the tekkie in the lab?

MISSION 3: TIME BOMB
What mystery is uncovered by the quake?

MISSION 4: HAMMERHEAD
Will the comet crash on Earth, destroying all life?

MISSION 5: SOLE SURVIVOR
Will a hostile takeover destroy the Mars Project?

MISSION 6: MOON RACER
Who's really controlling the spaceship?

MISSION 7: COUNTDOWN
Will there be enough time to save the others?

MISSION 8: ROBOT WAR
Will the rebels succeed with their plan?

MISSIONS 9 & 10 COMING FALL 2002

Discover the latest news about the Mars Diaries.
Visit www.marsdiaries.com